< donorboy >

VILLARD

NEW YORK

< donorboy >

> a novel:
>
>
>
>
>
>
>
>
>
>
>
>
>
>
> Brendan
>
> Halpin
>
>
>
>
>

All rights reserved under International and Pan-American
Copyright Conventions. Published in the United States by
Villard Books, an imprint of The Random House Publishing
Group, a division of Random House, Inc., New York, and
simultaneously in Canada by Random House of Canada
Limited, Toronto.

VILLARD and "V" CIRCLED Design are registered
trademarks of Random House, Inc.

LIBRARY OF CONGRESS CATALOGING-IN-PUBLICATION DATA
Halpin, Brendan.
Donorboy : a novel / Brendan Halpin.
p. cm.
ISBN 1-4000-6277-2
1. Accident victims—Family relationships—Fiction.
2. Fathers and daughters—Fiction. 3. Custody of
children—Fiction. 4. Mothers—Death—Fiction.
5. Teenage girls—Fiction. 6. Birthfathers—Fiction.
I. Title.
PS3608.A5493D66 2004
813'.6—dc22
2004043090

Villard Books website address: www.villard.com

Printed in the United States of America

1 2 3 4 5 6 7 8 9

FIRST EDITION

This one is for Rowen.

ACKNOWLEDGMENTS

After several false starts, I found the right way into this story after I spent an afternoon with Daniel Sokatch, Dana Reinhardt, and Noa Sokatch. Thanks to all three.

Thanks to Doug Stewart for continuing inspiration, advocacy, and friendship.

Thanks to all my friends in the English Department at Brookline High School.

Thanks to Bruce Tracy for excellent editorial support and encouragement, and for patience during the Great Title Search.

Thanks to everybody who read drafts and came back with praise and suggestions: John Andrews, Peg Halpin and the Pathetic Book Club, Dana Reinhardt, Andrew Sokatch, Daniel Sokatch, Sarah Strauss, and Jessica Yurwitz.

Thanks to Pamela Cannon for telling me four years ago that I was a writer rather than a guy who happened to write about something that happened to him.

John Mellencamp's *Trouble No More* helped me a great deal in writing the first third of this book.

Kirsten Shanks read every page as it was written and encouraged me when it was good, fearlessly told me when it was bad, and saved me from at least two disastrous wrong turns. She was my partner in writing and in life, and I miss her terribly.

< donorboy >

>
>
>
>
>
>
>
>
>
>
>
>
>
>
>
>
>
>
>
>

Okay, so here we go with my grief journal.

Jesus, that's mad corny. "My grief journal." —What are you doing, Ros? Oh, I'm just writing in my grief journal. Okay, grief journal grief journal, mad corny, mad libs, mad stupid, mad at the world (are you paying attention, Denise? Make sure to ask, why do you think you wrote mad at the world there?) I don't know, genius, maybe because my parents are dead and my dad is some dork and not Kurt Cobain or Bono or even that *Everybody Loves Raymond* dork or anything else I used to imagine, he's just a regular nonfamous dork like any dad, and I have absolutely no idea on earth why he would want me to live with him, I want to live with Aunt Karen, I want to die like Mom. And Mommy.

No, Denise, not really. I mean, I don't particularly feel like living now, because it seems really pointless, but I don't really feel like doing anything as big a deal as killing myself, and probably you don't want to hear this, Denise, but I don't really want to die a virgin, even though there's nobody I really . . . sorry, IM from Sasha, probably I should do this in a real journal instead of on the computer and it did cross my mind to say, "I have to go write in my grief jrnl :-[" but I was too embarrassed, it's too—see now when they ask what's hard about having two moms, probably the hardest thing is that when something is really really gay, like a grief journal, you can't say it's really gay, because that's like dissing my mom, who's dead . . .

Okay, fuck you grief journal and fuck you Denise, because I just sat here and cried for like ten minutes because my . . .

fuck.

I don't want to do this. Are you going to collect it, Denise? Am I going to fail grief? How did you do in grief? Did you ever take grief? What do you do when you go home? Do you have some dork that you love? Do you drive home and get crushed by stupid foodstuffs? I like that word. "Foodstuffs."

What the hell was I writing about before I cried twice. Fuck you Denise, fuck you Denise, I hate you Denise, I don't want to sit with the sadness Denise, I want to not feel like this ever, I hate Sean who I can't even call Dad because he's just the stupid donor, I can't even figure out why he wants me, especially since Grandma is all, "I'm just too old, honey," and Uncle Mike is all, "I have to work on some of my own issues right now."

Then again, Mom told me they didn't know the donor which is obviously a lie, so maybe the petri dish part is a lie too, maybe, ick, well, I can't even imagine this dork having sex with Mom, but then again the idea of Mommy having sex with Mom totally icks me out anyway, so maybe moms are just yucky and shouldn't have sex at all but then they wouldn't be moms, so there is what they call a conundrum, a dilemma if you will, impaled on the horns of the dilemma, killed by a truckload of turduckens.

Okay, IM from Sasha again, I guess she's nice to check on me, but I hate everybody worrying about me and talking about me and asking how I'm doing and how they all just look at me when I come to lunch because now I'm tragic, oh my God that is so sad, oh my God, I am so sorry, Oh my God Ros. Oh my God. I love them but I hate them and I wish they would shut up except when I don't want them to, but they always get it wrong.

I hate this, Denise. It doesn't help. Can I stop now? Please? Are you even going to read this?

> > >

You didn't read it, Denise, you just asked if I did it and how it made me feel and I really want to smack your fucking face when you ask me stupid shit like that or when I tell you how much I hate you and you say, "I know that you're feeling a lot of anger right now. Would you like to talk about that?" No, actually, I would like to smack your chubby cheek and see my handprint in red and watch the tears run out of your eyes and have you look at me and cry and ask me why why, it isn't fair, you only want to help me, you hate these ungrateful kids and then run out of the room and never ever come back and still feel the sting of my hand on your chubby little fucking cheek.

But that would mean something going my way for once, so instead you just do that annoying thing you do. "Let's talk about why you're feeling that way. How do you feel when you think about hitting me?"

I feel good, Denise. I feel real fucking good.

Ok, I'm lying. I feel like shit today and every day and I hate everybody.

I don't want to do this, Denise. I have nothing to say. Mom's still dead, and the last thing I said to her was some bitchy thing and I hate that, I hate you, I hate me, why does the last thing I ever say to her have to be some mean thing? I hate it, Denise, I can't stand to think about myself, I can't stand anything.

I don't have anything to say. I can't see the screen because I'm crying again.

This is a sucky idea, Denise. My grief journal is dumb, my grief journal is dumb, Denise is dumb, Sasha is dumb, Rosalind is dumb, and whatever fucking idiot invented the turducken is dumb. I think I'm going to go veggie just to protest. Also that should fuck with Sean, so that's good. He'll try to be all sensitive and pretend like he's not annoyed, but I'm like fuck you Sean, send me

back to Karen if I bug you, but you won't so I will make
you pay if I ever decide to talk to you. I guess I'm gonna
have to if I am going veggie. Or I could write him a note.
"Going veggie. Buy tofu. Hate you. Send me to Aunt
Karen." I think I smiled. Still my grief journal is dumb,
stupid, mad corny, mad mad mad.

> > >

Dear My First Grief Journal:
Still not talking to Sean. Sean is my dad. Sean is the donor.
Sean is some dork who lives in this house. I guess it's my
house now. I hate that. I hate this stupid single guy house
with the stupid big TV and PS2 and cable even though I
kind of like those things. I think I want to live in my own
house, in my real house, and I think I could stop the sale.
Then I could have my real room and my real door and the
thing on the trim in the kitchen where Mom marked how
I grew.

    But I guess Sean would have to live there too, and
Mom is never coming home, and Mommy isn't either, and
I know I would wake up every day thinking it was a bad
dream and I didn't tell my mom I hated her just before
she died because I couldn't go to some dumb party with
people it turns out I hate.

    I don't want to think about that. It makes me hate my-
self. Why can't I say I'm sorry? I'm so sorry, I'm so sorry,
please come back so I can tell you I'm sorry.

    Okay, other stuff, other stuff. Sean's house is weird and
boring. I want to go live with Aunt Karen.

Except I hate her too, I'm sick of her stupid phone calls, every night, honey is there anything you need, how you holding up kiddo, honey I'm feeling sad and missing your moms tonight, sweetie I'm really sad and I just want you to know that we are sharing that. Whatever. Take care of yourself, bitch. Nobody cares if you're sad, nobody cares if I'm sad, even stupid Sean who keeps looking at me like won't you please talk to me, and I just act like I don't even see that because the hell with him.

Denise, I really think this idea sucks. I felt okay when I started writing, and now I feel shitty and sad and I just want to lie on my bed and not sleep and wake up wondering where I am and then remember it all and dream about Mom at the foot of my bed saying honey I just want to check on you, I want to make sure you're okay, I'm sorry I had to leave. But she never says don't worry about being a bitch to me just before I died . . .

Goddammit Denise I have tears running down my face and big mascara streaks on my cheeks. Is this helpful? Is this a therapeutic dose? Can you just give me some drugs or something to make me feel normal? I don't want to cry anymore, I'm sick of crying every night and every day and when I'm peeing after C block and then while I wait for the T after school and I'm sick of everything.

And no I don't have any suicidal ideation, I learned that in my peer counseling training, isn't that funny? I was going to help those poor girls with issues. Because I really care. Those bitches look at me like I'm radioactive now. But I know all the questions to ask. Am I thinking about hurting myself? Only if raiding Sean's liquor cabinet

counts as hurting myself. Maybe it does. Do I have a plan
to hurt myself? I don't actually even know if he has a
liquor cabinet, and I don't want to do anything that might
cause me pain.

Maybe getting drunk would. Sasha puked really hard
last summer, but I was too scared, I didn't want Mommy
to get mad or disappointed, so I just held Sasha's hair
while she puked, and the sound of her puking made me
want to puke, but I didn't.

I'm not answering the IM's anymore. I don't want
to talk about how I am and I don't want to hear about
whether Andy likes her oh my God he looked at me oh
my God who gives a fuck.

> > >

Dear My First Grief Journal that Denise keeps asking
about and that I don't want to do but I'm still such a fucking goody goody that I won't stop doing because it's my as-
signed homework even though I stopped actually doing
my math homework isn't that funny?:

There's never any food here. I think I really am going
veggie. I thought it was a joke but I want to kill that pen-
cil neck on tv with his stupid yellow chickens even though
those might not be the turducken chickens, but anyway, I
can't eat any meat without thinking about how it comes in
a truck that overturns and kills somebody's mom.

So I did leave a note. I left out the hate you part. It
said, "Sean. I am a vegetarian. Please buy food. There is
never any food here." and I didn't sign it. When I got

home from school the next day the house was completely packed with food. Organic everything in the fridge and every cabinet packed with organic vegan stuff. He even bought those horrible fruit-juice sweetened cookies that Mom always . . .

Anyway. I guess I should have been touched or something, but it just made me want to smack him. Like I just had to say jump and he would say how high and that is a pathetic loser of a 35-year-old unmarried man who will do that for a 14-year-old.

He left me a note. It said, "Rosalind—Bought food. Will microwave one organic burrito of your choice in exchange for five words. Think it over."

I've got his five words right here.

>>>

To: Rosalind90@aol.com
From: Sean_Cassidy@publaw.org
Subject: Five words

Dear Rosalind:
Well, I guess Did You Fuck My Mom is, in fact, five words. I hope you enjoyed the burrito. Mine was cold in the middle.

So listen. Or, rather, read. I have taken your five words as an invitation to tell you some stuff about me. I'm going to send you something every day at my lunch hour. Maybe you'll write me back sometime. Maybe you won't. Maybe you'll talk to me. Maybe you won't. In any case, I hope you will at least read what I write to you and not delete it. I guess I don't know if you will or not.

Okay, so I am sorry that I was choking on black beans and soy cheese in a whole-wheat tortilla when you asked your question and so didn't get to answer it. My standard comeback when somebody swears unexpectedly . . . well, never mind. Anyway, I thought about getting indignant, like what happens between two adults is none of your business, blah blah, but it is the beginning of your life we're talking about, so I guess the question is fair.

Sorry I am going on at length and still not answering the question. This is what lawyers do, I suppose.

Anyway, I did not have sexual relations with that woman. (That's a Bill Clinton joke, but maybe you are too young to get it. That is a kind of scary thought to me. But anyway.)

Here's the deal: I took the Red Line to the Green Line, got off at Brookline Village, walked into this eight-story glass box of a building, took the elevator to the fourth floor and walked into Fertility Solutions, suite 416. I went by myself, though I had tried to get Marcia, who was my girlfriend at the time, to go with me. (This little fact becomes important later. Bear with me.)

I signed in with the receptionist, and then a nurse, a heavy, fifty-ish blond woman who sported that olfactory treat of too much perfume covering up cigarette smoke, and had gold rings on every finger and fingernails that were probably an inch and a half long and a name tag that said "Angela" escorted me to the donation room and handed me a clear plastic cup with a blue lid. I placed my donation in the cup and returned the cup to Angela, which was probably the most embarrassing moment of my life up to that point. I don't know exactly what process followed, but a month later, Sandy called to tell me that Eva was pregnant. I was jumping up and down I was so happy. Marcia was there, and she was less happy.

So that is how you were conceived. I guess it's not that much of a story, in the end. But since I am your father, sort of, I mean, bio-logically definitely, but anyway, I think it is my parental responsi-bility to bore you with stories. So you didn't ask, but I'm going to tell you anyway about how I met your moms. I know that after my mom died I liked hearing stories about her. Except when I didn't, and then I wanted to throttle the stupid insensitive jackass who was trying to tell me some stupid story about my mom that was more about him anyway.

I guess if I'm honest, those are the kind of stories I have to offer. Like I said, you can read them or not. But I hope you do.

Love,
Sean

> > >

Dear stupid grief journal that seems unfortunately to be my only friend these days:
Well, well, well, Sasha has stopped with the IM, and she is pretty much not talking to me at school anymore, which is probably because I am likely to bite her head off about something stupid mostly because I hate her for having parents, which is not really her fault, and at lunch the other day I had to leave when stupid Sara started bitching about "I hate my mom, blah blah." I hate Sara's mom too, I mean, I get why she hates her mom, her mom is a total nightmare, but still it's better . . .

I don't know. I'd say the same thing if I was her, and then I probably wouldn't notice if the girl whose two

moms just got crushed by foodstuffs got up and ran to the
bathroom and cried while some druggie girl smoked Marlboros in the next stall.

I don't know what her name is, but she offered me a
smoke, and I almost took one because what the hell, it's
not like I have to worry about what Mom would say, or
how Mommy would launch into how Grandpa Ed died of
lung cancer. Which, I mean, if you look at it, she died with
clean lungs, but not smoking didn't keep her alive. Nothing keeps you safe ever, so why bother trying to stay safe
ever, why do anything to stay alive when you could die
today?

I am not crying. I don't know, O, Grief Journal (we
read that stupid poem where he goes "Go to it, O
Jazzmen" in English class, and it was the dumbest, but I
do kind of like that O, and I can't very well say O, Denise,
since Denise told me she's never going to read this, Okay
Denise, whatever, maybe I'll just stop writing it then.)

But then who am I going to talk to? Sasha? Kristen?
Sara? They're all, I have to go do homework so I get into
Harvard early decision, and I'm all I stopped doing math
homework because my mom died and so did my mommy
and geometry seems pretty unimportant next to that, I'm
sure even Ms. Weymouth would agree. Prove these trian-
gles congruent: 1. Axiom, life sucks. 2. Fuck you. 3. Trian-
gles are congruent. Maybe I could talk to that druggie girl
in the bathroom, which is I mean, I guess if you are smoking Marlboros in the bathroom something's gotta be
wrong with you, and something's wrong with me too, and

it was nice how she offered me a smoke even though smelling like shit probably wouldn't have helped my day any, but she didn't want to talk and relate, she didn't want to distract me, she just offered me a Marlboro, and those are like eight bucks a pack or something, so it meant something for her to offer me one.

I'm still not crying. I guess that's what I wished for. But I don't feel anything right now. That's better than feeling bad, I guess. I remember that girl I was, who hung out with Sasha and Kate and Sara and Kristen and thought about stupid stuff and cared about stupid stuff and worried sometimes if she would be gay like her moms, which I guess wouldn't be so terrible, but now who cares? Why even bother being gay, why bother not being gay, why bother with anything. Why bother eating. Because I'm fucking starving and it turns out I really like those burritos Sean bought.

> > >

To: Rosalind90@aol.com
From: Sean_Cassidy@publaw.org
Subject: Why me?

Dear Rosalind:
Don't worry, I don't mean why me as in "Why me? Why me?" which is a Nancy Kerrigan joke you almost certainly don't get unless you were following the Olympics closely at the age of three.

That is to say, this is not an e-mail about why bad things happen

to good people, or to anybody, or anything. Did anybody tell you
God has a plan? They used to tell me that.

But, as I said, this is, rather, an e-mail that will try to explain a
little bit about why I am your father, or why Sandy and Eva picked
me to be their donor.

It was 1987. I had just finished my first year of college in
Boston, and I didn't feel like going home to Philadelphia. This
was . . . well, my dad was a bartender, smoked a lot of weed, and was
really more of a roommate to me than any kind of parent, and a
kind of messy and annoying one to boot. I suppose a lot of guys my
age would have enjoyed that situation, but I figured if I wanted a
bartender roommate, I could probably find one on campus who (a)
didn't smoke and aggravate my asthma, and (b) didn't listen to
Emerson, Lake and Palmer obsessively and give weekly lectures on
the underappreciated genius of the *Tarkus* album.

So I started checking the bulletin board at the student union
for sublets, and ended up on the first floor of a house right on a
busy traffic rotary, living, as luck would have it, with a guy who
worked as a bouncer at a bar in Ball Square. My roommate, Dave,
didn't smoke and owned no recordings by Emerson, Lake and
Palmer, his taste running more to Loverboy and Triumph. This was
not too great in my opinion either, but he worked all night and
slept all day, whereas I had to get up at six every morning, so we
basically never saw each other. That proved to be the basis of a
friendship that endures to this day, which actually appears quite
strange when I see it written down.

I found a summer job at a different university across town as a
kind of camp counselor at Future Dreams, which was basically summer school for middle-schoolers from the Boston Public Schools. I

led most of the group activities, supervised the homework time, organized the Friday field trips (incredible pain in the ass), and led the Friday field trips (usually very fun). Sandy worked as a teacher in that program. I should tell you that the students really liked her. They used to complain to me about everybody else, and they never had a bad thing to say about Sandy. This is doubly impressive because they always made it clear that her class was hard and they thought she gave too much homework. Also, she had this spiky short hair and wore a pink triangle pin all the time (which is what they had before the rainbow flags, but maybe you know that). I probably don't have to tell you that middle-schoolers are not the most tolerant people on earth, but they never made fun of her or even said a word about her being a lesbian. I didn't get this at the time, but of course that meant that they really liked and respected her.

I hope my talking about your mom is not going to bum you out. I can certainly stick to talking mostly about myself if you prefer. Blink once for yes, twice for no. I'm kidding. Sort of.

At the end of the summer I got invited to the first of the annual end-of-summer blowouts, which I assume they kept having after you were born, but I guess I don't really know. I wanted to go, but I was a little afraid. I was young and it was, remember, 1987. So pretty much everything I knew about anybody gay came from *Three's Company*, where Jack wasn't even really gay but just pretended to be. Do you even have any idea what I'm talking about? I guess if Sandy and Eva had cable you might have seen an old episode sometime.

Sandy was the first avowedly non-heterosexual person I had ever known, and though I liked her, I was kind of afraid of her in

the way I was afraid of Jehovah's Witnesses. Not that I thought she
was going to knock on my door and try to convert me, but just
that I thought she belonged to a strange world I knew nothing
about whose members might possibly hate me.

When I got to the party, Sandy introduced me to Eva, and I
pretty much lost all power of speech. Again, I don't know how much
you know about *Single Dads Club* or Eva's years as Tracey—it
seemed like it was not something she really obsessed about even
at the time, so maybe they never even mentioned it. In any case, I
had had a terrible crush on your mom, Eva, when she was on *Single
Dads Club* during my sixth- and seventh-grade years.

Just in case you don't know the basic outline, Jim the skinny
dad and Gary the fat dad had to room together with Jim's wise-
cracking ten-year-old boy and Gary's ostensibly teen daughter (actually a 21-year-old Eva at the series' beginning). Hilarity and a
large number of Very Special Episodes ensued. Tracey gets drunk.
Tracey's best friend attempts suicide.

There's really no explaining why I was obsessed with this particular girl on this particular sitcom—it was not any better or worse
than any of the other crap on TV at the time—maybe it was just
that it was on on Wednesday nights, when I usually needed a boost
because the weekend was coming, which, when your dad's a bartender, is not something you look forward to. Whatever the case, I
watched it religiously for both seasons it was on, and I was left
hanging for life about whether Tracey was going to go backpack
across Europe with her hippie boyfriend or go to the University of
Michigan like her dad wanted her to.

They never aired the continuation of the "to be continued"
episode about Tracey's big decision. I turned on the TV the follow-

ing Wednesday, and *Love, Sidney* or *The Fall Guy* or *The Facts of Life* or something was on, and I never found out what happened to Tracey.

So, as I said, I met Eva, and my brain immediately liquefied. Because she was Tracey. Is this icky? Too much information? I guess most people kind of take it for granted that their fathers had crushes on their mothers, but I accept that this is new and possibly gross information for you, so I will skip ahead.

It was a really fun party, and like about twenty other people there, I ended up spending the night. (How much am I supposed to admit about my alcohol consumption? Well, I suppose if we ever establish any kind of relationship at all, it will probably not be based on your belief that I am some all-knowing perfect sage, so I might as well just tell the truth and hope my honesty scores some points. I got completely hammered.)

And then I remember waking up with an elf wielding Mjolnir, the Mighty Hammer of Thor, beating at my skull from the inside. (That is both a comic-book joke, which I assume you don't get but made anyway, and a hangover joke, which I sincerely hope you don't get.) I was on the couch. Apparently this was lucky, as I had to step over several people sleeping on the floor on my way to the bathroom. Where I vomited.

I washed my face, swished some water in my mouth, and staggered into the kitchen. And then I began to clean. Luckily I was the first one up, so I didn't have to explain about how a morning-after party scene Activates My Childhood Issues, since, as I said, Dad was a bartender. Saturday nights when I was in middle school I would stay up and watch *Saturday Night Live* and then go to bed. He would return a few hours later, occasionally with coworkers, but more often with some drunken woman he had picked up at work.

When I got up on Sunday morning, I cleaned up the beer cans, Chinese-food containers, pizza boxes, joints, and whatever other detritus covered the living room floor before I even had my first bite of Honeycomb.

This was pretty much the routine up until I left for college, and would probably be the routine now, except, of course, that I am no longer there to clean and Dad is getting a little long in the tooth and has that foggy idiocy of the long-term cannabis addict that the ladies may not find as beguiling now as they did in 1980. But, to be fair, I don't actually know. I don't go to Philadelphia very often.

So the long and short of it is that I spent an hour picking up garbage from Sandy and Eva's lawn simply because I couldn't stand the sight of it. I filled two big garbage bags by the time the elf decided to put Mjolnir down and start banging away with just a standard-issue sledgehammer. I went back inside with a bag over each shoulder and found Sandy and Eva at the kitchen table.

They were pleasantly surprised that I had undertaken some cleaning and were only too happy to supply me with some baking soda as a reward.

I mixed myself a nice antacid shake and enjoyed the rest of the morning reading the paper while the rest of the overnight guests gradually staggered into the kitchen.

So this was our first real social contact, and the beginning of our friendship. Looking back, though, I think this may have been a key event in my path to donorhood—yes, I was, like everyone else at the party, completely inebriated, but unlike anyone else at the party, I also cleaned up first thing in the morning. I may well be delusional, and they never really went into detail with me about their rationale for choosing me, but they certainly knew many men, and I am the one they chose, and perhaps it sounds

strange and pathetic that I am proud of that fifteen years later,
but I am.

More to come.

Thanks for listening.

—Sean

>>>

To: Sean_Cassidy@publaw.org
From: Rosalind90@aol.com
Subject: Re: Why me?

Do you ever work?

>>>

Dear Grief Journal:

Her name is Jen and I guess I'm gonna have to start smoking if I'm gonna hang out in there but anyway I went to
the bathroom at lunch not to cry but just because I was
hoping to see Jen again and that sounds kinda gay but gay
in a lesbian way not in a grief journal way. I don't know
if I have a crush on her. I guess I'm scared I do. Which I
thought I wasn't scared of being a lesbian anymore but I
guess that survived anyway. Hooray.

Still not crying. Haven't cried since lunch yesterday.
I don't know if that's good or not. I feel like I'm full of
concrete.

So I went in and peed and she was there again and sit-

ting on the windowsill smoking Marlboros and not lights
because those are girly, Sara's mom smokes those. I kind
of can't stand my so-called friends anymore because they
were friends with somebody I'm not, some goody-goody
girl which I still dress like but don't feel like inside. And
which I guess has something to do with me not doing my
math homework and not even trying to scam anybody like
boo hoo my mommy's dead can you give me an incomplete,
which is totally what Sasha would do, but in the end I just
kind of don't care if I fail everything because what's the
point, so there's no use trying to scam people into letting
me get over because like I said I don't care if I get over.

I'm trying really hard not to think of Mom or
Mommy during the day, but then even at night when I try
to think about them I can't cry. I am kind of writing here
to see if I can cry because everything I write always comes
back to Mom or Mommy and I can hear their voices, no
wait that's Sean playing Metal Gear Solid 2 in the living
room because I'm pretty sure Mom never said, "Snake?
Snaaaaaaaaake!" Hey Sean that is a video game joke
which I think you might get since you are playing that
video game now. Dork.

Anyway, I was talking about Jen and I did ask for a
smoke because like I said I wanted to hang out with her
not Sasha and stupid people at Our Table, I think I used to
think of it like that with capital letters, but now it's Their
Table because I'm not part of any Our except maybe for
Our Window Ledge and Our Marlboros though I didn't pay
for them and when I went to buy cigarettes after school I
bought some Camel Reds because I thought I should at

least have a pose if I'm going to smoke, plus I didn't want
to look like this dork freshman trying to be like the junior
girl even though of course that is what I am.

The cigarette was gross and I did cough like it was my
first one which it was but it did feel cool kind of to sit on
the window ledge and blow smoke out for one thing because you could totally fall out. Also when I got out Sasha
looked at me all prissy and worried and was like "Oh my
God, Ros, were you SMOKING?" like I just killed somebody. I lied and was like "no there were like random drug-
gies smoking in there." Which I guess means I am not as
much of a smokin' bad girrrl as I thought I was, not yet
anyway.

Jen says her mom is a drunk who hits her dad a lot.
She says school is wack and that is certainly a point of view
I am coming around to as everything that used to seem im-
portant to me is now kind of amazing in its wackness.

I told her right away that I had these two lesbian
moms who just died because I thought if she was going to
be a bitch about that like some people are then we should
get that out of the way. She said she was sorry but not in
that "Oh My GOD" way like she was psyched to know
someone tragic because it was good drama which is I'm
sorry the way all my "friends" are and probably what I
would have done if Sasha's folks had been crushed by
foodstuffs.

I am tired and how dumbass is this but I am going to
smoke a cigarette because I don't want to look like I don't
know how in the bathroom at lunch tomorrow.

>>>

To: Rosalind90@aol.com
From: Sean_Cassidy@publaw.org
Subject: Why Me, Part Two

Dear Rosalind,

I do occasionally work, though given what they pay me around here, I should probably cut down. That is a public-interest lawyer joke.

Speaking of cutting down, I realize that I am not exactly in a position to be very parental with you at this point, so I will not tell you that you shouldn't smoke, but I will ask you to please not do it in the house. The entire house smelled like an ashtray last night, and I am convinced that the olfactory disturbance was key to my lack of success at Metal Gear Solid 2: Sons of Liberty.

Having said all that, I am glad that what you are smoking is just tobacco. Or should I not tell you that because that will make you go roll a joint just to spite me? I am very new to this parenting thing, and my coworkers with teens have a great deal of advice to share with me, but given the uneven results they seem to be experiencing, I don't really put much stock in their advice. Furthermore, I do not know if I occupy an important enough place in your life for you to want to do something to spite me. Is this something I should aspire to? (Sorry—that is a rhetorical question.)

In any case, this is my second and final attempt to explain how I made sense of why your moms chose me.

We now fast-forward to my third and final summer at Future Dreams. I never really kept in touch with your moms during the year, because I didn't really feel comfortable calling up because I thought they'd think I had some big crush on Eva. This of course was correct and will be my final reference to this fact because I know it's icky. Also, I was a college student and they were adults with real lives.

I returned to Future Dreams every summer while I was in college, and Sandy was always my best work friend. We sat together at meetings, and I went to the big party at the end of each summer. I was supposed to do the Future Dreams end-of-the-summer gigantic blowout trip to Lake Paradise Amusement Park with this woman Helen, who was this incredibly uptight English teacher who carried around both the student and staff handbooks, and would always quote from them extensively and who got me in huge trouble because I let the students use their Walkpersons walking to the cafeteria.

I got Sandy to switch with Helen, so the two of us were the chaperones for the Lake Paradise trip. I should say that this was an impressive gesture of friendship on your mom's part, as everybody hated this trip because of the two-hour bus ride there and the two-hour bus ride home as well as the impossibility of supervising middle-schoolers effectively in an amusement-park setting.

I will spare you most of the details of this trip, though they are permanently engraved on my memory. Here is the relevant part: at the end of the day, both Nick and Andre vomited copiously after their fifth cotton candy and seventh ride on the Eliminator, which, by the way, is a fantastic roller coaster. Perhaps we should go sometime, if you wouldn't be too humiliated to be seen in public with me.

Please refrain from comment on that last part.

When Nick and Andre vomited, they managed to cover most of my shirt and shorts in pink vomit. I took them to the bathroom and cleaned them up, and I heard Sandy yelling for me before I could clean myself up.

She was in a bit of a state, which I am sure is a state you have seen her in, and she announced to me that Kadeem and Kyanna were missing, and the look on her face also pretty much reviled me for making her come on this trip.

Since Sandy was freaking out, I felt the need to stay calm. Since I was with the kids during all their free time, I knew that Kadeem and Kyanna couldn't keep their hands off each other and had probably gone off in search of a place to make out. Still covered in vomit, I went from ride to ride asking the operators if they'd seen the happy couple and we eventually found them inside the carousel.

In any case, I proved myself competent in a crisis. A week later Sandy invited me over for dinner, and after a bottle of wine, she and Eva told me how they were eager to reproduce but were missing a key ingredient, and they asked me if I'd be willing to supply what was missing. I agreed, and here we are.

Gotta go. I actually do have some work to do.

—Sean

    > > >

To: Sean_Cassidy@publaw.org
From: Rosalind90@aol.com
Subject: Re: Why Me, Part Two

Aunt Karen says they picked you because you were smart and because Mom had found out over three summers that you didn't have any serious diseases in your family.

Dear Grief Journal:

Sean is a goober. He is also a pathetic goober with no life
and no wife and no girlfriend that I can see. Now here is
another conundrum for you: would it be worse for me to be
a lesbian like my mom and have somebody who loved me
who I could die next to (trying, but can't make myself cry
even by writing that) or to be a straight loser like Sean who
I still don't think of as my dad, who probably has lots of
porno here somewhere because there are no live women.

I guess Sean could be gay but he made such a big deal
of saying how he had this crush on Mom, so even though
the house is really clean I think he is probably straight.

I had an okay conversation with Aunt Karen because
for once she didn't talk about how she was sad and she kind
of agreed with me that Sean is a goober and said that she
would take me in a second but she doesn't have the money
for a custody battle and anyway his name is on my birth
certificate as my father which I don't really understand
why Mom did it if he was just supposed to be the donor.

School is still wack. I really think I might skip every
day if I had any idea of what I could do that would be any
better or more fun. I am totally not afraid of getting in
trouble because who gives a shit if Sean is mad or disappointed in me, and anyway he didn't even seem to care
that I was smoking which just shows he is no kind of parent anyway. And also, what could possibly happen to me
for skipping school? Am I suspended? Expelled? I can't
imagine that any of those things would matter to me be-

cause what's worse than losing both your parents in an accident that people snicker about when you aren't in the
room because it involved stupid foodstuffs?

I am already sick of Denise. I told her about school
and about Jen and about being afraid of being a lesbian
and about how I'm not crying and all she ever does is ask
me questions. How do you feel about that? Why do you
think that is? What makes you say that? Why don't you
shut the fuck up, Denise? I am totally skipping my next
appointment. Why do you think you want to skip our next
appointment? Because this isn't helping, because I can't
cry anymore which I thought I didn't want to cry anymore
but now I feel like it means I am a bad daughter or something and you can't give me any advice or tell me anything
about how to do this. What would you like me to say? I'd
like you to tell me it's okay, or it's not okay, or I shouldn't
smoke, or that I should do my homework, that I am
wrecking my life, tell me something!

Do you think you are wrecking your life? I think I'm
going to kick your ass. I don't know if I have a life to
wreck, but I know that the house sold for six hundred and
fifty thousand dollars and that that money is mine when I
turn eighteen, and so it's not like I really need to bust my
butt to make sure I get a good job or anything, and anyway
I could die tonight, but I don't think I will. But if I did die
tonight and I had my nose in a geometry book, wouldn't I
think I'd wasted my life? I don't know. What do you think?
Why do you think you keep mentioning geometry?

Because I fucking hate geometry, Denise! Arrrgh! I
am totally skipping next week.

> > >

From: Sean_Cassidy@publaw.org
To: davidsanders@Newcastle.k12.mass.edu
Subject: Over My Head

Dave—Don't worry: It's not "Over My Head" like the Fleetwood Mac song, but, rather, over my head as in I don't know what the fuck I'm doing here. Rosalind appears to hate me, which is, I suppose, normal, or to be expected, or something. She was smoking in her bedroom last night. I did nothing but write her some ridiculous e-mail about how her moms chose me because some kid vomited on me at Paradise Lake.

No, that's not a joke. It's actually what I wrote. I wanted to unsend it as soon as I sent it, but of course you can only do that on interoffice e-mails. So she wrote some snide response fueled by Karen, who also appears to hate me, though from what I have seen of that woman she is in no emotional shape to take care of a grieving teen.

Of course, I am hardly winning awards in this category myself. Other than hooking her up with Denise and pretty much making her go, and providing a large stock of frozen vegan burritos (they are actually surprisingly good, and I recognize that coming from Mr. Bachelor Cuisine that recommendation might not mean much, but they really are tasty), I am just exactly the kind of dad to her that my dad was to me, which is to say none at all; I am simply the roommate who happens to pay 100% of the rent.

I thought that taking her was the right thing to do. I certainly could have allowed Karen to take her. Perhaps I should have. I am wrestling with the idea that I took Rosalind for purely selfish reasons—to try to fill up the gaping hole in my life, to make me feel like my life is not a complete waste, to help me forget about my lack of success with the ladies since Marcia (could that be counted as a success? I suppose the jury is out). And so what I undertook for selfish reasons now just reminds me what a loser I am. Far from filling the hole in my life, it's reminded me of how huge and well-defined that hole is and how my pathetic attempts at being a dad are not filling it.

I am sorry to annoy you with pathetic whining. I have actually tried spreading this stuff around, but both Ian and Stephanie only ever make me feel worse, so you're elected. Note that I did not call you, because I knew that you would yell at me to shape up and that you would be correct to do that, but I just wanted to revel in my loserdom here for a few minutes.

Keep on rockin'

—Sean

> > >

To: Sean_Cassidy@publaw.org
From: davidsanders@Newcastle.k12.mass.edu
Subject: Re: Over My Head

Sean—Snap out of it! Shape up! Since I didn't get to tell you on the phone, I thought I could at least give it to you on e-mail.

Did I get from your e-mail that you have been writing to her about why her moms chose you, which is something you don't actually know anything about beyond one half-drunken conversation?

Why not tell her why you chose her? Doesn't that seem like it's actually more important information to her? Though I hid it well behind a wall of "oh my God, don't do it, don't do it, you are insane," I was actually moved by what you told me about why you wanted her. Maybe she will be too. Or maybe she'll murder you while you sleep. What do I know about what's important to a fourteen-year-old girl? Eight years till Max gets to that age, and if he's anything like me, he'll probably still just want stuff with Spider-Man on it. And pornography.

Superhero porn—we'd have the teenage-boy market sewn up. I'll put together a business plan and get back to you. Keep ya head up,

—Dave

> > >

Dear Grief Journal,
Goober, goober, gooberific, dorktastic, Sean is a loser. Tried to talk to me tonight and I was just acting like I didn't even hear him and I could see him getting mad which I kind of liked.

But then I felt kinda bad about the fact that I don't have anybody to talk to so I sent Sasha this IM and I was all like I'm sorry I've been such a bitch and she was all yeah you have been but it's cool, and I was like, well, I didn't write this but I was like oh sorry if my grief is inconvenient for you, and then she tried to write some dumb thing about English class, which I guess she didn't notice that I have been sleeping through.

Westerberg tried to talk to me about it after class, all I

lost my parents too and I'm trying to give you space but I
don't want to add failing English to the problems you have
right now, and I wanted to say, yeah, *you've* got problems,
dude, like the fact that your class is a joke and I could
sleep through it and still get an A, but I didn't.

I always think of this really mean shit to say and
then I don't say it and I don't know if that's good or bad
because I pretty much feel mad all the time, so maybe
if I really unloaded on Sasha or Westerberg or Sean
or Karen or anybody but Denise it would help me not
feel so grumpy all the time. Or maybe if I went back
in time and got in the car instead of saying whatever
Mom, I'm staying home where it's less corny, then I'd
be dead. But what's funny is that even though I don't
really enjoy life very much I find that I don't really
want to be dead.

Because for one thing you can't smoke when you are
dead and the smoking is definitely coming along, and
now I start feeling kind of itchy during D block just
waiting for the smoke, so that's good. Jen is always there
and I told her about Sean and about how he is a dork and
Jen was like well my dad is a pussy who lets my mom
beat him up and I said well I bet Sean would probably
kill to get that close to a woman which is a mean thing
I actually said because it wasn't about the person I was
talking to.

Progress reports go home this week. I wonder what
Sean will say when he sees that I am failing everything
but English. I am passing English only because I read
everything which is more than most of the humanoids in

that class do. Or should I call them homunculi, which is another great word I learned from actually doing the reading. If I cared at all about sucking up I would have slipped that in when I was talking to Westerberg, all "I hate the homunculi in this class" or "how can I stay awake when some homunculus is asking a dumb question every two minutes."

But anyway, Sean will probably send me some other really wussy e-mail about how he doesn't feel like my dad but he's concerned. Whatever, loser.

Speaking of losers, let's talk about the girl who can't cry because her moms are dead. Still nothing on the tears front, it's like I am bored with everything except maybe smoking which is still too new to get boring and Jen who is also somebody new, but basically I am just bored bored bored and I really hate everybody including me, because what kind of daughter am I anyway. Mommy would kill me if she found me smoking. She'd be "in a state" as Sean put it, hopping up and down, all red in the face, all do you know what you're doing, are you trying to hurt me don't you know how my dad died?

I'm sorry, Mommy, I'm not trying to hurt you, I just needed an excuse to stay in the bathroom. Except maybe I am trying to hurt you because I am mad at you too, I am mad at you two, that is an interesting homonym, or is it a homophone, but anyway you left me and you didn't make any plans for me at all and so all of a sudden I have to be this grown-up who figures stuff out when I just want to be an idiot teen like Sasha and Sara and Kristen and pretty much everybody else.

I'm sorry I said that Mommy I don't know if you can read this or hear what I'm thinking or anything. I'm not mad, I just want you back. I just want you back.

Progress—I felt that itch in my tear ducts even though nothing came out. But I did make myself sad, and how fucked up is this but that kind of makes me happy.

> > >

To: Rosalind90@aol.com
From: Sean_Cassidy@publaw.org
Subject: Me and You

My friend Dave told me I was an idiot for sending you an e-mail about why your moms picked me (I did not tell him that I actually sent two), since, as he correctly points out, I don't exactly have firsthand knowledge of their decision-making process. I am sure Karen is probably closer to the mark than I am; that would certainly explain why Sandy was always steering our conversations around to hereditary illnesses. Once I found that your grandfather Edgar had died of cancer, I decided Sandy had some hypochondria issues, but the idea that she was vetting me by asking if I knew anybody with Prader-Willi or St. Vitus' dance makes more sense. (I don't know if she actually asked me about those two, but they are illnesses that sound kind of funny to me. Though I dare say they probably are not funny to have.)

So Dave suggested I tell you what I told him when I was decid-ing to take custody of you. I don't like any of my verb choices for that action: "take custody" sounds awfully stiff, while "exercise my parental right" sounds good to my lawyerly ears but leaves out the significant emotional component.

To wit: I looked at you and I saw myself. I don't mean any kind of physical resemblance. I mean a biographical resemblance.

When I was nine years old, my parents were probably on the verge of divorcing. Mom was in her first year as a public defender, and Dad was in his nineteenth year of the 1960s. At the time I didn't really know anything about the relationship between my mother and father; I just knew that Mommy was busy and that Dad worked at night, so they never saw each other. This is probably why they stayed together as long as they did.

Both my parents had been hippies in the sixties, but Mom seemed to be following the idealism thread of that decade by becoming a public defender, while Dad seemed to be following the substance-abuse thread by working as a bartender and weed dealer and consuming a rather significant amount of his own merchandise.

One evening Mom was on the platform waiting for the subway, and, it being rush hour, there were several hundred people there, so no one was ever able to clearly discern what happened, but apparently there was some jostling, or an altercation between other people, or something. In any case, someone bumped into her and she fell and hit the third rail and died immediately.

I remember waiting with Dad and watching him get increasingly angry and frustrated and talking to Mom out loud when he thought she was just late from work. He was angry and talking about how inconsiderate she was, and how he was going to be late for work. Then the phone rang and he got that look . . .

I'm sorry—I thought I could write about this in detail, but I find that even twenty-six years later, it hurts too much. It never really hurts any less; it just hurts less often. I don't know if that's a comfort to you. I was certainly not comforted by anything anyone said to me in the weeks and months after Mom's death. I was especially angry with my aunt Maureen, who told me that God has a plan. I wanted to tell her that if God's plans include taking a nine-year-old kid's mommy away, then God is a sick evil fuck, but I would not have said that at the time. Indeed, while I knew those words, I wouldn't have put them in that order. But the idea was there. Perhaps you feel something similar. Perhaps you don't. Perhaps I should be more circumspect in my choice of language with you. As I am making this fatherhood stuff up as I go along, I will make mistakes. Perhaps swearing is one of them. But if your high school is anything like mine, you hear much worse in the halls on a daily, and indeed probably hourly, basis.

Well. To wrap up. I saw in the paper that your mothers had died, and I cried and cried for you. Or possibly for myself at age nine. In any case, I remembered being a little kid and missing my mommy and having essentially no parent, which sounds cruel to my father, but he simply didn't do any parenting. I wanted to do anything I could to help you because I know something about how you feel and I know that you don't deserve it, and because I love you. Perhaps tomorrow I will tell you about when I first saw you. So when Eva's lawyer called and told me that she had died intestate and that my name was on your birth certificate, I really wanted to finally become your father instead of the donor.

So far, with the exception of the burritos, I appear to be doing a horrible job. I am mindful of the irony of my complaints about my own father given my own abysmal performance, and so I have two things to say to you as I sign off:

1. Please please please stop smoking.

2. I have received your progress report. I myself was an indifferent student who became academically driven after my mother's death, so I am not surprised to see a major change in this area. Nevertheless, I am concerned that your failing everything but English will close some important doors to you, so you and I will meet with your guidance counselor after school on Wednesday. This will, unfortunately, force the cancellation of your session with Denise this week, which I am sure will take some of the sting out of having this kind of meeting.

By the way, I spoke to Denise, who informed me of your desire to "kick her ass" and skip your next session. After speaking with her for twenty minutes, I have a certain amount of sympathy for your point of view on both issues. Please let me know if you'd like me to find you someone else.

I picked up several frozen enchilada meals from the same company that makes the burritos. I can only hope that they will rise to the high standard set by the burritos and that you will join me in finding out tonight at seven. Meet me by the microwave. I will be wearing a Boston Red Sox hat and a gray T-shirt.

—Sean

> > >

To: Sean_Cassidy@publaw.org
From: Rosalind90@aol.com
Subject: Re: Me and You

Don't worry about the fucking swearing. Why the fuck would I care about that shit?

ps—I think God is a sick evil fuck.

pps—Yes, please find somebody else, I really do hate Denise.

ppps—Thanks.

> > >

To: davidsanders@Newcastle.k12.mass.edu
From: Sean_Cassidy@publaw.org
Subject: Breakthrough?

Well, Rosalind spoke to me last night. Now, this was certainly not
any kind of long, involved conversation—basically I heated up
some frozen enchiladas and we ate in silence as usual, and she said,
"Thanks for buying these. They're good." And I said, "No problem. I'm
sorry I don't really know how to cook." She said, "It's okay. We used to
eat dinner like this all the time. You know, always a ton of stuff to do,
everybody's got work and committee meetings and soccer practice
and whatever. No time to cook, no time to eat. We ate a lot of pizza."
    "Well, yes, I suppose that's pretty much how I eat too."
    "I guess a lot of people do. Well, I have some reading to do. I'm
going to my room."
    "Okay. Thanks."
    "Yep. See ya."
    Now, I grant you this is not much in the way of a conversation,
but after all that stony silence, it feels pretty wonderful. I was over
the moon all night. I hope this is the beginning of a trend.

—Sean

>>>

Dear Grief Journal:

Well, Sean is still a dork but at least he got me an appointment with someone named Lisa who is some kind of adolescent expert or something, or so he claims, and so Denise
is gone which is okay, but I guess I really don't know if she
sucked as bad as I think she did or if I just hated her because she made me think about stuff I didn't want to
think about and asked really annoying questions all the
time. Maybe they all do that. I guess I'll find out if Lisa
does or not.

So I guess we have this big deal meeting with Mr.
Mould about my lack of academic progress or whatever. It
is funny because I am not scared at all, and that kid I was,
that kid with the two moms would have been terrified, but
I'm just like what the hell could you possibly do to me?
Well, whatever, I don't know. I really don't want to be
some burnout loser, I mean I did used to like getting A's
and feeling smart and making Mom and Mommy proud,
but now I don't know. I don't want to study. Or do anything else. I told Jen about my meeting and she told me
that they will probably say the words "therapeutic setting," because I guess she has a meeting about every other
week where they try to get rid of her and that's what they
say to her all the time, or her mom or whoever, but anyway she told me a bunch of words that Mould will use and
told me I should make a little bingo thing in my notebook
so after he says "Therapeutic setting" and "not achieving
to her potential" and maybe something like "very con-

cerned because we consider ourselves a family here" I can
check them off.

Ugh. I still haven't cried. Jen says she stopped crying
too, that she used to cry every time she heard her mom
and dad fighting, or anyway every time she heard
yelling and her mom slapping the shit out of her dad,
that she had this little room in her house she used to go to
to cry and rock back and forth holding her knees, but now
she just sits in her room and watches that plastic surgery
show on cable and it's just like the normal background
noise. It's like people who live next to the airport who
don't hear the planes taking off anymore. Anyway, that's
what Jen says but I don't know if she actually knows anybody in East Boston or if she's just kind of using that as an
example. Also she is smoking in the bathroom at lunch
and having therapeutic setting meetings, so maybe she
should cry and not watch that show, even though it is actually kind of good. I've watched it a couple times before
Sean gets home from work while I am not doing my
geometry homework.

I wish I could get some kind of grief-oplasty and be
like that kid who got her ears pinned back, all "the kids
called me Dumbo and now I am happy and have an ugly
prom date because I got my ears pinned back." Could I be
like "I used to smoke in the bathroom and hang out with
this girl who kind of scared me but I also liked and also I
used to fail everything, but then I got my grief redacted
and now I am going to the prom with some mullet-headed
loser who will try to cop a feel in the limo!"

I want to be with Jen all the time. But I don't really feel

like I want to kiss her. I don't know what that means. Maybe Lisa the adolescent grief queen can tell me if there's some kind of lesbo checklist or something. I guess I could ask Aunt Karen. I don't know. I love her and everything but I think she still thinks I'm this little kid and I don't know how I would ask her how she knew, when she knew or what. I think I might have been able to ask Mom and she would have been cool about it, but then we get back into the icky thing about moms having sex or even thinking about sex and so maybe I wouldn't have even asked.

I am tired, tired of being me all the time.

> > >

CHARLESBOROUGH HIGH SCHOOL 10/07/04.

INFORMAL MEETING.

Participants: Rosalind Butterfield, Sean Cassidy, Richard Mould

SEAN CASSIDY: Is it okay with you if I record this? It's one of those lawyer things.

RICHARD MOULD: Sure. Is that some kind of digital thing?

SC: Minidisc.

RM: So you get, what, about eighty minutes on a disc?

SC: Something like that. If my batteries hold out. (*Laughs.*) Once I had to take this deposition (*pause*) well, never mind.

RM: So, before we begin, I just want to turn to Rosalind here and ask if you have anything to say before we begin.

ROSALIND BUTTERFIELD: No.

RM: So I have here, and Mr. Cassidy I've made copies for you, e-mails from all of Rosalind's teachers. (*Pause.*) You can see that it's much the same thing across the board. With the exception of English, which is a notable bright spot. All of your teachers, Rosalind, are very worried about you. (*Pause.*) Right now you are not on track to pass anything but English this quarter, though Mr. Stinson says if you pass the constitution test, it is still possible.

(*Pause.*)

SC: So she could still pass history and English for first quarter.

RM: Yes. Now, of course, failing for the first quarter is not necessarily destiny in terms of failure for the year. But I do need to tell you both . . . well, Mr. Cassidy, we consider ourselves to be a family here, and we're frankly very concerned about Rosalind's success. As I said, it's mathematically possible to fail the first quarter and pass the remaining three, but I have to be honest with you and say that I don't see it happen very often.

SC: Well, in the cases where you do see it happen, what makes the difference?

RM: Well, of course a variety of factors—

SC: I am a little concerned about what I'm hearing here, because it sounds to me like you are writing off Rosalind's ninth-grade year here based on four weeks of grades. It just feels premature to me.

RM: No no no, not by any means. But I would like to just have you keep an open mind about all of the possibilities here. We all hope that Rosalind will turn things around, but down the road, if she doesn't, it wouldn't hurt to consider the idea that a therapeutic setting might be more appropriate given the nature of the trauma—

SC: Are you suggesting that you can't meet Rosalind's needs here?

RM: Well, we are unclear right now about exactly what Rosalind's needs are, but it is clear she's suffered a terrible tragedy, and while we certainly will continue to do our best for her here, we may find down the road that she needs more of an intervention than we are equipped to provide.

SC: Well, she is going to counseling.

RM: Which is fantastic, but it seems to me that Rosalind may have some issues that she is working out that may supersede her academic—

RB: Bingo!

RM: I'm sorry?

(*Silence.*)

SC: Rosalind, what are you doing there? Is that a buzzword bingo game?

(*Silence.*)

SC: Now, when we do this at diversity training at work, you actually have to raise your hand and work the word *bingo* into your comment. I mean just to shout it out like that—

RM: (*Clears throat.*) This is the kind of behavior that—

SC: Yes? Have you had complaints about Rosalind's behavior?

RM: Well, not as such, but her teachers—

SC: Are very concerned about her, as you said. So am I, but I have to tell you that I find the content of this meeting frankly disturbing from both a personal and professional standpoint.

RM: I'm sorry?

SC: Well, Mr. Mould, Rosalind and I were under the impression that we were here to talk about solutions, to try to move forward, and you've opened with the suggestion that Rosalind find an alternative placement. It seems to me that should be the very last thing we consider.

RM: Well, no, I am not suggesting that a therapeutic setting would necessarily be more appropriate, but I do think we should investigate all of our options down the road if it becomes clear that Rosalind is not succeeding here. I'm just trying to open the conversation so that if, down the road, we reach that point, we'll have a clear idea of what we're looking at.

SC: Is this district willing to foot the bill for a therapeutic setting?

RM: Well, most of our parents naturally choose private facilities that—

SC: Yeah, yes, I'm sure that they do. And the district pays for these settings?

RM: Well, on a case-by-case basis we review the—

SC: Mr. Mould, I'm sorry, I wonder if I can just talk to Rosalind privately here for a moment?

RM: Certainly.

(*Sounds of papers shuffling, door closing.*)

SC: So, let me see what you've got: "consider ourselves a family," "therapeutic setting," "investigate our options," "issues that supersede," "down the road." Well, you really shoulda put that one at least twice. You were briefed for this meeting, huh? I mean, you knew what was coming?

RB: Yeah, I guess.

SC: I wish you would have told me. If I knew this guy was this full of shit, I never would have wasted our time coming in here. (*Silence.*) Ros?

RB: Don't call me that, okay? It sounds weird coming from you.

SC: Fine. Rosalind? (*Silence.*) We're on the same side here. You know? (*Silence.*) Did they make you read *A Man for All Seasons* in English? (*Silence.*) You should read it. There's a whole thing in there about how silence implies consent. Thomas More tries to use it as a defense to stop Henry the Eighth from cutting his head off. Anyway, so if I say, "We're on the same side," for example, and you say nothing, for example, we can take that to mean that you assent to the statement.

RB: Whatever.

SC: Do you want to stay here?

RB: You mean now?

SC: I mean do you want to keep going to school here? Because I think this guy is an idiot, and you should stay here just to spite him, but if you'd rather start over somewhere else, we can do that. I just want to help you get what you want here.

RB: Yeah, you care a lot about what I want. Drop me off at Karen's then.

(*Silence.*)

SC: Okayyyy . . . Well, I guess we're done here.

END OF RECORDING

> > >

To: davidsanders@Newcastle.k12.mass.edu
From: Sean_Cassidy@publaw.org
Subject: Counselor meeting

Good afternoon. I've just returned from a meeting with Rosalind's
guidance counselor, which, apart from providing the food and shelter, was supposed to be my first official real dad act and ended
horribly. The guidance counselor essentially wants me to put Ros
in some kind of group home for troubled teens, and Ros doesn't
want me to call her Ros and wants to live with Karen.

I really didn't know what to do, and it just went horribly. I
started getting all lawyerly with the counselor, which didn't appear to make any progress, though I thought up a good line to use:
"Do you understand that I sue schools for a living?" But I want to
save that one for something special.

In any case, it's clear that Rosalind is having a hard time with
her grief, and I appear to have hooked her up with a real dud of a
therapist, at least to start with, and the school is just flummoxed.
I suppose they have fifteen hundred kids there and just have nothing in place for the small percentage in crisis, but it really made
me angry. The counselor made it clear that Charlesborough is not
a school for kids with problems.

So, at the end of the day, the counselor is angry at me, I am
angry at him, and Rosalind appears to be angry at both of us.

Then again, she pretty much appears to be angry at all times,
but her playing the Karen card seems to indicate a spike in her
anger level.

I am once again finding that I have no talent for this parenting business, which may be why the eligible bachelorettes have been less than inclined to stick around in the last few years. Do you think they have some sort of radar about that? Well, given the number of troglodytes who father children, I suppose the answer there has to be no.

Ugh. Please tell me that this is going to get better.

—Sean

> > >

To: Sean_Cassidy@publaw.org
From: davidsanders@Newcastle.k12.mass.edu
Subject: Re: Counselor meeting

Hmm . . . so the counselor was a tool and the teen was sullen? Sounds like every parent meeting I've ever been to. Seriously, I go to like five or six of these a year, and if you didn't scream at anybody, you did good. I've seen parents look like they were about to hit their kids and also sat there for twenty minutes with the counselor and the kid and no parent while the kid looks at us like, "Well, failing stuff to get attention was evidently a bust." But I have also seen people who appeared normal and loving hit a brick wall with their kids. Nobody knows what to do with teenagers, and most administrators are dicks. Give yourself a break.

I don't know what to tell you about the bachelorettes and why they haven't stuck around except what I've already told you a million times. I will say that whenever I am at the playground with just Max, there are many opportunities to mingle with the single moms if I wanted to, so maybe taking Rosalind in will pay some un-

expected dividends, like you will meet some nice woman when you
are both bailing out your kids or something.

That was supposed to be a joke.

Call me later.

—D

> > >

Dear My Favorite Grief Journal:

Hey I never noticed this but when I typed that the computer tried to make it say Dear Mom and Dad which
would be a funny kind of letter for me to write.

Well, Lisa is much better than Denise, she will at least
say stuff to me, I mean say not ask, so when I said I was
sort of worried about the lesbian thing she said something
I had to stop listening to because it bored the shit out of
me but basically I think she said that's not something I
have to make up my mind about right now or really even
ever.

And when I told her that I can't cry she said that was
normal and probably me trying to protect myself but that
it will happen and it doesn't mean I don't love my moms
or maybe I guess I should use the past tense there.

Today I was thinking about them a lot. I miss them
a lot even though I can't cry about it. That was probably
why I was a bitch to Sean even though he kind of stood up
to Mould which I did appreciate because he is a dick. But I
was like if they were still alive I would be getting A's and
Mould would barely know my name and they'd come

home from parent night all "your teachers say the most wonderful things about you" and all that stuff and I was sitting there in that meeting like I just slipped out of my own nice life and into somebody else's crappy one. That's not really Sean's fault, I don't think he made the turduckens, but it is his fault he took me instead of giving me to Karen which probably would have been the humane thing to do but then I probably would have had to change schools since she lives in Dedham and who the hell wants to live in Dedham.

But I did kind of change schools already because there is a whole school here that I never knew about but I actually walked into the caf to get some fries and saw Jen and her friends sitting at a table and they kind of motioned me over and I got all like I think I blushed or something but I went and I was really happy to go and to see how Sasha and Kristen and all of them looked at me like quickly looking and pretending not to look and then huddling close so they can talk about how I'm a druggy now, which I'm not even though I had lunch with Bitches With Problems. That is what Kate said anyway and she is an artist who shoplifts or that's what Jen told me. But when I sat down Kate was like welcome to the Bitches With Problems table and I was like, okay, I guess I fit both categories. Nobody asked me what my problem was. Maybe Jen told them already, but even still they didn't look like they wanted to talk about it and they didn't ask me anything about oh my god how am I doing and I liked that.

I used to look over at this table just the way I noticed people looking at this table today, like there go the freaks

with the weird hair and clothes and too many piercings
and the fact is that they have been way better to me than
my own non-druggy friends the bitches without problems
or anyway the bitches with different problems, but I
shouldn't even say that because Kristen anyway is very
nice and I do know that Sasha was trying, it wasn't like
she didn't try.

So I guess except for the fact that I am still an orphan
living in some strange guy's house, things are looking up.
Except I still haven't done any work in geometry or history or earth science or espanol unless you count watching
Dos Mujeres, un Camino which I did for like ten minutes
last night with the captions on so I could read the words
but I still didn't understand it. But I am pretty sure one
of the mujeres is in love with that guy with the long hair.

> > >

To: Rosalind90@aol.com
From: Sean_Cassidy@publaw.org
Subject: The First Time Ever I Saw Your Face

That subject line is a Roberta Flack joke. She also did "Killing Me
Softly," which was a big hit for the Fugees a few years ago. Of
course, now that I think of it, you were only five or six when that
came out, and so you might not even know what I'm talking about.
Lauryn Hill . . . well, never mind.

The meeting certainly was a disaster. Of course, as I look at it
now, I am not certain what I hoped the meeting would accomplish,
except to show you that I care about the fact that you are failing

everything. Except English. I have no idea if it was a success in that respect and if knowing that I care might be counterbalanced by the fact that your counselor obviously doesn't.

In any case, should we ever have another meeting at school (perhaps it could be something along the lines of "Rosalind has really turned it around!"), I would deeply appreciate it if you could share your intelligence with me. That way I will have a better idea of what to say. Also I might be able to compete with you on the bingo front, which always makes it more entertaining. I won during the last diversity training, having put "baggage" in nearly every square. I raised my hand and said to the facilitator, "When you described the cycle of oppression, I thought about this Haitian client that I just couldn't connect with and I thought, 'Bingo! That's it!'" There were audible groans from my co-conspirators.

Well. Several days ago I promised to tell you about the first time I saw you, so here we go with that. After you were born, I went to the hospital and saw you with your moms. Looking at it objectively, of course, you were a baby much like every other baby, but I couldn't believe what I felt. I looked at you in Eva's arms and saw the most perfect, wonderful baby ever in the history of the universe. This may sound corny and unbelievable, but I honestly felt like my heart would explode. It was the strongest emotion I have ever felt, tied with intense grief, which is saying something.

I am at a loss as to how to explain this, but feeling that much love is terrifying. I was very young, and therefore terrified of the responsibility of raising a child, but I was also terrified of the way looking at you made me feel. It was an entirely positive feeling, but, well, as I said, it was terrifying. I hope you will get an opportunity to experience the same thing. But not soon. In any case, your

mothers and I had essentially agreed that I was not going to be a
real parent to you. I always assumed that I wasn't really supposed
to participate—that in addition to the lack of St. Vitus' dance in
my family history, my youth was a positive factor in my selection
because it implied that I would not try to be your father. That
sounds unfair to your mothers, so let me say the following things.
First of all, when they asked me what I envisioned my role to be, I
panicked and mumbled something about how I wasn't ready for
any kind of responsibility. My memory is that they appeared relieved at this answer, but I may be projecting my own relief that
they accepted my answer well. They did say they would leave the
door open should I change my mind. Once I actually saw you, I was
terrified of the strength of my emotion, so I went to law school
and worked hard and didn't socialize with anyone, and eventually I
fell out of touch with your mothers. This was my own doing. I didn't
know how to conduct myself around you, and, as I said, I was
frightened, so I backed off. I do believe that they were sincere
about the door being open to me having more of a role in your life,
but I never walked through. I am sorry about that. When I reflect
on my life I see a series of missed opportunities, and that is certainly the greatest one.

Your mothers wrote to me every year on your birthday with a
picture and an update on how you were doing. I rarely wrote back
but always appreciated the letters. I still have them if you would
like to see them. They are in the black photo album on the bottom
shelf in the living room.

Well, I do have schools to sue here, so I must return to work. My
coworker Ramona informed me that there is a new and delicious
vegetarian restaurant a mere ten minutes out of my way on the
way home. I will come home bearing takeout tonight, so don't fill

up on enchiladas. (I found them somewhat of a letdown after the pleasant surprise of the high-quality burritos. Well, I guess nobody bats a thousand . . .)

—Sean

> > >

To: Sean_Cassidy@publaw.org
From: Rosalind90@aol.com
Subject: Re: The First Time Ever I Saw Your Face

I know you care about me failing everything. The only problem is that I don't. I actually kind of wish I did, but I don't.

Don't be so hard on yourself about not being around. I am actually not trying to be mean, but it's not like I missed you, if you know what I mean. I had two great parents which is more than a lot of kids have.

You are right about bingo. Next time I am putting "down the road" like three times. Unless next time actually is down the road, in which case I don't know what he would say. That is a conundrum. I will ponder and get back to you.

> > >

4/15/94

Dear Sean:

Here's a copy of Rosalind's preschool picture. She is doing wonderfully well—still a little shy with the other kids, but the teachers love her, and she does have a couple of good friends in her class. They come over here for play dates sometimes and play house for hours. It is very cute and also a little scary to hear our words coming out of her mouth when she is being "mommy." "Now, honey, you are getting all wound up! Do you need a time-out?"

She has a bike with training wheels that she likes to ride, but she is still afraid to go down hills. So we have to put the bike in the car and drive to the Arboretum where it's flat.

She will begin kindergarten in the fall, but after two years of preschool, I don't think it will be too much of an adjustment. I do worry about her being shy in new situations, but both Sandy and I were shy too, and we turned out okay.

Finally, she always makes up songs that make us howl with laughter. Yesterday she sang this one that went something like, "Oh, when we go to P-town this year . . . I hope we don't have a house with a leaky roof . . . that Mom will say I can't believe what we paid for this fleabag flophouse . . . and it doesn't rain every day . . . because I hate playing Sorry."

I have no idea if that's funny if you can't hear her singing it. In any case, she is a delight, and she makes us laugh every day.

Love,
S&E

> > >

Dear Journal de dolor:

Good news, I think, which is that I randomly opened the black photo album and read some thing about when I was four and I cried and cried for like twenty minutes, big loud crying like the neighbors probably could hear, and I am still really sad which feels horrible but better than feeling nothing at all.

I miss them so much so much so much. I really really want them back right now. I feel the great big horrible hole that is like right in my stomach where they used to be or where I used to keep the love they gave me or something, but it hurts, and that is partly because my throat hurts from crying and my stomach hurts because I was bending over, and my shirt has snot on it because it was roping out of my nose and I didn't care, just kept crying and crying. I felt horrible and I still feel horrible, and I know I wanted this but I don't like this either.

I know it's stupid to ask why why did this happen, why me, why them, I don't understand why they died, I don't understand why I didn't. If I came along would I be dead too, or would we all be alive because they waited for me to put my shoes on or something, and the turducken truck killed somebody else or better yet nobody.

Nothing makes any sense. Lisa tells me I can't think about what ifs, that I will drive myself crazy, but if you could die because of some stupid decision, how can anything be important ever? Or not important? How do you ever know if you are making the choice that is going to kill you?

I guess you just choose things that feel good and say

fuck it. Except nothing feels good right now, nothing at all feels good. I HATE THIS! HATE IT! Crying again, I hate my life, I hate everything, I hate everybody I hate this stupid fucking horrible sad life and I want my real life with my moms who love me back! Why can't I have it back?

> > >

Dear Fluffy:

I told Lisa about how corny the idea of a grief journal was, and she agreed that that was a pretty stupid name but said it sounded like it was good for me to write in it, so I could call it whatever I wanted. So I chose Fluffy. Mom's friend Rick had a lizard he called Fluffy and I always thought that was kind of funny, and so here we are with me and Fluffy, which maybe is lizardlike because it is ugly and unpleasant but I kind of like it.

So I don't know what to do about the black photo album. The black album. I think that's a Metallica record, or that's what Kate the Shoplifter said, but she said she likes *Ride the Lightning* better. Which I don't care about but I am writing so I won't have to think about my black album and whether I should read any more of what Mom and Mommy wrote about me, which I kind of want to but also don't. It made me too sad but I know there are thirteen more of them in there and I really want to read them all but it's like picking a scab or something. It's kind of fun, but sometimes you don't feel like bleeding again. Ooo, I am poetic. That is what you call an extended metaphor, and I know that so I am not failing English. Nobody really

mentioned that I am getting a C— because I ace all the
terms and vocabulary tests without studying but I never
write the papers because who the hell wants to do that?

Anyway, besides the Black Album, I am invited to a
party this weekend, because Sara's parents are going out of
town, and Sasha came over with Kristen to invite me and
they were all we really miss you and we're sorry if we
made you mad or whatever and I felt bad for ignoring
them and writing all kinds of mean shit about them because it looks like they at least care about me even if they
bug me sometimes, and we had this big girly crying hug
which was corny but felt nice anyway.

Of course Sara's house is in east buttfuck and I don't
want to hitch a ride with some drunk person who will
crash and kill us both or get us arrested or whatever. I
should probably just tell Sean I am spending the night at
my friend Sara's house, but I don't know what he would do
or if he would want to call or something queer like that
which would be mad embarrassing, so I think I am going
to sneak out and go to Kristen's and have her sister drive us
because he never comes in here once I lock myself in, so it
should be all good.

I hope. I don't know how it's going to feel hanging out
with them again. More like me, or more like who I used to
be? I don't know but lunching with BWP is nice because
they don't ask me about stuff but all the same it might be
nice to hang out with some people who are happy sometimes too.

>>>

Dear Fluffy:

I am in some deep shit, and I guess I don't care. Apparently Sean knocked on my door last night because he saw something about Mom on TV, not like I wanted to see that shit anyway, some kind of tragic update on E! about how a former sitcom star was killed by turduckens, but anyway, he called Karen, he called the police, and when I got home this morning all I wanted to do was puke and sleep and I had to listen to him yelling at me about how he had the police out here and how worried he was and why didn't I just ask him and blah blah blah.

He called Karen and she wanted to put me on the phone and she bitched me out too, all did I know how worried she was and on top of Mom and Mommy dying she doesn't want to lose me too, and blah blah blah and I was like it's all about you, but I didn't say that, I just said sorry to her, which I didn't say to Sean even though maybe I should have because he looked bad like he did really worry about me but if he didn't knock on my stupid door he wouldn't have even known I wasn't there, and I need a better lock for my door or something because you can pick those doorknob locks with a bobby pin, which he didn't have but I guess he found something.

Whatever whatever, I am a big disappointment, I am a big pain in the ass, I hurt people's feelings, I am a horrible person, well, so what anyway, I had a really good time.

Everybody was there, and unlike last summer I was not too scared to drink so I drank something clear that tasted kind of like a nasty Sprite or something, but I guess I was pretty drunk because I did pass out last night or fall

asleep or whatever, and then I woke up this morning with
my legs all achey and I had to puke and Sasha held my
hair like I did for her last summer and it was like old
times or something. I guess I also had some elf in my
brain with a hammer or whatever Sean's dorky hangover
joke was. It is now four in the afternoon and I am just
starting to feel normal, or sort of normal, but I didn't
like the way I felt this morning but I felt really good last
night, like I was really happy and my head was going to
float off my body or something and I didn't think about
being sad or feeling sad or anything. It was just like I was
right there the whole time and I didn't have to worry or be
sad about anything and I could laugh and laugh which I
haven't done in a long time.

I talked to this guy Chris for a while. He is a junior
and he is some kind of skateboarder or something, which I
always see those guys trying to go down the railing by the
library and laugh because they always fall on their butts,
but he was cute and nice and he gave me some stickers
that he and his friends made. Once he gave them to me
I recognized them from being on every pole and I asked
him what the design was, kind of expecting him to say
something stupid about freedom or his skateboard or
something, but he just said he thought it looked cool.

I'm not sure if I wanted to kiss him, but maybe I
would have if I hadn't passed out. So I maybe want to kiss
him but not really spend all my time with him because
that would mean less time with Jen who hasn't exactly
invited me to a party and told me she cares about me
but who I still want to hang out with all the time. I don't

know where that puts me on the lesb-o-meter. But whatever, I don't have to decide, I can kiss whoever I want and
that is pretty cool I guess.

I want to get drunk again, but maybe not that drunk
because I hated the way I felt today, but I felt better last
night than I have since . . . But now I am grounded or
whatever, but I don't really know how he can stop me
from sneaking out my window. And he unhooked my
internet, all, you can't send IM's anymore and I was
like who cares.

I am going to take a nap which I haven't done since I
was like four years old but I am tired from everything.

> > >

To: davidsanders@Newcastle.k12.mass.edu
From: Sean_Cassidy@publaw.org
Subject: Failing

Dave—Jesus, but we had a horrible horrible weekend. I actually
did try to call you, but apparently your cell phone was out of range.
I hope you had a good time at the wedding. In any case, my subject
line here refers to my progress as a father.

Rosalind disappeared into her room as usual on Saturday night,
and I really thought nothing of it. At about nine-thirty, I was flick-
ing around the channels, and I came across some little report
about Eva, just a little video obit, so I TiVoed it and called to Rosalind. I wasn't sure if she'd want to watch it, but I thought I should
give her the option.

She didn't answer me, so I knocked on her door, and she still

didn't answer. Eventually I picked the lock and went into her room.
I have no idea if that is ethical or not. In any case, she wasn't
there.

I called Karen, who took the opportunity to verbally abuse me,
and some friend of Rosalind's, whose mother, after asking if I was
That Shaun Cassidy and confessing a teen crush on That Shaun Cassidy, told me she thought her daughter was at my house. Wonderful.

I panicked and called the police, which made me feel like I was
doing something. The cop came out and filed a report and told me
she had probably sneaked out, "to meet up with some boyfriend or
other, don't panic, my daughter did it too, which is why I'm forty-
eight with a ten-year-old grandson, ha ha, but we got through it."
I believe he was actually trying to reassure me.

Finally she showed up at eight in the morning obviously hung
over. I yelled at her, which did not seem terribly effective, so
I called Karen and got her to yell at her, and she at least got
an apology out of her, which seemed like a victory, though
of course I was angry and jealous that she hadn't apologized
to me.

I already drove a couple of screws into the window frame so it
won't open wide enough to allow her to escape. Thank you again,
by the way, for the cordless drill, which helped immensely. I did this
at four a.m. in a fit of pique when I was convinced she had sneaked
out. At five I was convinced she was dead, and I cried.

I don't know what I should be doing differently. I actually
thought things were starting to turn around. Since our big breakthrough enchilada conversation we have what I suppose is almost
normal parent-teen interaction, which is to say we talk briefly
about the logistics of daily life. "Does this smell funny to you?" and
"We're out of Frosted Mini-Wheats." We've talked briefly about our

shared hatred of her school, and the other day she actually sat with me to watch TV. There was some commercial with a mother and son holding hands in the sunset or some such nonsense, and my eyes began to fill up as they always do at mother-son commercials, and she saw me and said, "So you weren't kidding. It really never stops." And I said, "Well, I can usually restrain it to the trickle down the cheek these days, which is actually a significant improvement." And she said, "Well, hey, life may suck now, but it looks like I've got a lot to look forward to." And we both laughed. We laughed together!

I know, I know, cue the strings and the shot of us gamboling into the sunset, but it was really a wonderful moment.

And now I have to be the prison warden. At 3:43 I was actually considering driving to the twenty-four-hour Home Despot to see if they had any razor wire. I settled on the screws instead.

I am a horrible father and I don't know what to do.

Thank you for your attention.

—Sean

    > > >

To: Sean_Cassidy@publaw.org
From: davidsanders@Newcastle.k12.mass.edu
Subject: Re: Failing

Oh my God, she snuck out and got drunk? Anybody would think you've got a teenager on your hands!

Seriously, man, relax a little bit. I see a lot of teens and the one thing I have learned is that they all drink and have sex, except the

ones who smoke weed and have sex. The first few times I was surprised when I would overhear something or find a note or whatever,
but now I am always surprised if I find out they don't do that stuff.

You're trying, which, believe me, is a lot more than a lot of people do. I'm sorry it's so hard, though. She will be fine. She is going
to do some stupid shit, because she's a teenager and that's what
teenagers are supposed to do. Of course, when Max hits his teen
years I am fitting him with one of those tracking ankle bracelets
and putting saltpeter in his food. And yes, professor, I know that
doesn't really work.

I don't know what to tell you except that the fact that she went
to a party and got drunk just shows that she's fourteen and not
that you are a terrible dad. I mean, you may actually be a terrible
dad, but this doesn't count as evidence.

Congrats on the laughter, dude. That is actually huge, so I won't
bust your balls about how you are a sentimental ninny.

—D

> > >

To: davidsanders@Newcastle.k12.mass.edu
From: Sean_Cassidy@publaw.org
Subject: Re: Re: Failing

Sentimental ninny, eh? Let us not forget the conversation we had
after Max's birth. Just in case you might have forgotten it, I have
the transcript here somewhere . . . Let's see . . . "I can't see from
crying, I'm just so fucking happy, it was so fucking incredible . . ."
"Most important thing I will ever be a part of . . ."

In any case, Rosalind appears to be contrite for her drunken es-capades, or something, because I have seen much more of her in the last few days and she has actually been overall quite pleasant. Please don't tell me that means she is plotting something, because I have already thought of it and I am choosing to take the more pleasant, less cynical interpretation.

I expected her to be angry about the screws in her window, but instead she seems to find it funny and has taken to calling me "Warden," but in a way that feels kind of affectionate.

Last night we had what I believe to be the first real conversa-tion of our lives together. She said, "So, Warden, where are the ladies? I mean, you know, there don't seem to be any ladies coming around. Did I scare 'em off?" It appeared to me that she hoped that was the case.

And so I explained how Marcia left, though I downplayed that the fact that I had fathered a daughter by another woman ap-peared to have been the catalyst, or rather the issue that caused her to reject my proposal. I further explained how my luck since then has been abysmal for reasons I don't fully understand, even though you keep telling me that I keep falling for Marcia over and over in different guises.

Before I even knew what was happening, I very cheesily asked if she had someone special at school. She looked at me as though that was the corniest, most embarrassing, most awful thing I could have possibly asked her, and this shot me back to my dad asking me something similar when I was her age, and how I screamed at him and slammed my door. Fortunately, she did neither, but said, "Well, you know, I have kinda had other things on my mind lately."

I am not buying that for ten seconds, but I was impressed with the graceful escape. She is an impressive kid. We have actually had several conversations since then that feel a great deal like real conversations.

I would very much like to get to know her better, and I am therefore currently in search of some sort of bonding activity. Since cleaning vomit out of the bathtub was about the extent of my adolescent bonding with Dad, I am hoping you might have some suggestions. Did you and your father stick up liquor stores together, or share steroid needles or something?

I am feeling good enough to bust your balls, so I suppose that means that things are looking up.

—S

> > >

New text message!
From: Rosalind cell
12:34 pm
IN TRBL. NT MY FAULT. PRNCPL CLLING U. HES A TOOL. WILL MAKE U BNGO CARD.

> > >

CHARLESBOROUGH HIGH SCHOOL 10/27/04.
INFORMAL MEETING.
Participants: Principal Steve Vanian, Sean Cassidy, Rosalind Butterfield.

SEAN CASSIDY: Do you mind if I record this? It's just one of those lawyer things.

STEVE VANIAN: Well, as we discussed on the phone, this is not
a formal hearing, that will take place in three days, uh,
this is more—

SC: Yes, I understand. But I'd like to record this all the same,
if that's okay with you.

SV: I suppose that's fine. Is that a minidisc?

SC: Yeah, I—

SV: Yes, I thought so. That's what Scott Simon from NPR
used when he was here last year. Maybe you heard the
series?

SC: No, I—

SV: "What's Right with Public Education"?

SC: No, I—

SV: It aired on *Weekend Edition* on four successive Satur-
days.

SC: Yes, well, if we could—

SV: Scott was here for the better part of a week, and
he seemed to be changing the minidisc all the time.
Still, the sound was fantastic on the radio—sounded
just like I was in the room. Which of course I was,
ha ha! Strange experience, hearing yourself on the
radio.

SC: I'm sure. Now you'll forgive me, but I was a bit flustered
when you called, and if you can just walk me through
the procedure here one more time.

SV: Of course. As you know, we have a mission here at
Charlesborough High School to educate the leaders of
the twenty-first century, and integral to that mission is
the maintenance of a safe environment here in the
school building.

sc: Yes, Dr. Vanian, we are aware of the seriousness of what Rosalind allegedly—

sv: I'm sorry, Mr. Cassidy, but there simply is no allegedly about it. There is a boy in the nurse's office with bandages all over his broken nose, and had our crack custodial staff not cleaned the blood up already, you could see the rather gory scene that awaited me when I arrived in Room 411.

sc: Yes, I am sure it was a very gruesome scene, and when we return for the hearing in, what?

sv: In three days.

sc: We'll get to the bottom of exactly what transpired. Now, did I understand you correctly on the phone that this will be an expulsion hearing?

sv: That is correct.

sc: Now, is this standard procedure in a fight situation? Because your handbook states that a three-day suspension is the standard punishment for a fight, and so I am just curious as to what makes this fall outside of that procedure.

sv: Well, if there is a weapon involved, that falls into a more serious category, assault with a dangerous weapon, and as we are dealing with a particularly egregious unprovoked act of violence, it's my feeling that we need to take this course of action in order to protect the safety of the learning environment here at Charlesborough High.

sc: I'm sorry, but you mentioned a weapon?

sv: Yes, in this case, a shod foot.

SC: A shod foot.

SV: Correct. As the second blow was administered with a shod foot, that clearly falls under the definition of a dangerous weapon in Massachusetts. And I need to tell you that any action the school takes is distinct from any legal action that the Commonwealth may choose to pursue. Pursuant to our procedures, I have informed the Charlesborough Police of the incident, and they will be coming to take statements. Should the Hoffmans choose to press charges, there may be serious legal consequences.

SC (*Whispering*): You actually had "a shod foot."

ROSALIND BUTTERFIELD: (*Unintelligible.*)

SV: I'm sorry?

SC: I'm sorry, Dr. Vanian. I just needed to go over something with Rosalind.

SV: As I'm not certain you fully grasped the seriousness of what I said, I will repeat.

SC: If the Hoffmans press charges, Rosalind is headed for DYS lockup. I got it.

SV: Mr. Cassidy, I really don't think your nonchalance here is at all appropriate. Because as the educational leader of this institution, I am forced to take seriously any threat to the safe learning environment here, and I need to tell you that this is a situation we are taking most seriously.

SC: Yes, Dr. Vanian, we are taking it seriously too. But I know my daughter, albeit less well than I would like, but I suppose any number of parents might say the same, um, but anyway, I am confident that once I get Rosalind's side of this story, I'll say, "Bingo! Now I understand!"

RB: Damn!

SV: I'm sorry?

SC: Well, Dr. Vanian, if that's all for now, I will take Rosalind, and we will see you and . . . Superintendent Boon?

SV: Actually it's Assistant Superintendent Watt.

SC: Fine. Well, see you at the hearing on Thursday at . . . ten?

SV: Correct.

(*Sounds of papers, walking.*)

SC: It was "educational leader."

RB: Yeah, I gave you the one that had "safe environment" twice. Shoulda kept that for myself.

SC: So. You wanna tell me about it?

RB: I don't want to cry here. Can we do it later?

SC: Yes, but given that we only have three days to try to keep you in school and out of lockup, I think we ought to.

RB: OKAY! God! We can talk about it when we get home! Jesus! (*Pause.*) Are you still recording?

SC: Oh, yeah thanks, I

END

> > >

STATEMENT OF MR. ANDREW WESTERBERG

Upon the end of my D period class, a group of four or five students stayed behind. They were talking and laughing.

As I was erasing the board and entering attendance in the computer, I was not aware of the content of their conversation.

I heard a scream and turned around to find Jim Hoffman on the ground with blood streaming from his nose. Rosalind Butterfield, a student in my E period class, was standing over him and, as I ran to the scene, kicked Jim in the thigh.

I restrained Rosalind. It is my opinion that she would have struck him again had I not intervened. I directed a student to fetch the nurse and another to contact Dr. Vanian.

I asked Rosalind what happened, and she replied, "Tell him to shut up."

> > >

Dear Fluffy:

Lisa says I should write about it so I can "try and make sense of it for yourself before you have to go defend yourself." She was nice about it. And Sean even though I kind of hate to say it was very cool in the meeting which helped because I was actually kind of scared. Which is funny because when we met with Mould I was all like who cares, but this seemed like it was more serious which I guess it is because they could lock me up. But Sean says he asked somebody he knows and they said that they never lock you up for a first offense, they just give you a parole officer and make you go to school, except I don't know where I'm going to go if I'm expelled except maybe some kind of special school for violent troubled teens, which is

not what I think I am but considering I broke that kid's
nose and I guess I smoke and drink, or at least smoke,
maybe the shoe fits, if you know what I mean.

Which I am still not writing about it because I can't
believe he said that and I don't want to have to write it
down or think about it or anything. But I don't know,
maybe Lisa is right and it will help and even stupid
Denise was right about the writing sort of, so here I here
I here I go.

I walked into English and heard this stupid kid who
I don't even know, I mean, whatever, I guess I know him
now, and he is a junior and he is a total dick, but anyway,
I just heard him talking to his friends and he was like, "I
keep watching E! just hoping they'll show that again, I
swear to God I was laughing my ass off, two dykes crushed
by meat!"

What's weird and I guess kind of scary is that I don't
remember making the decision to punch him or anything,
it's just like I was looking at my fist and it was hitting the
kid's nose and it made this sick crack and then I kicked
him and then Westerberg was grabbing me probably trying to cop a feel, no not really.

It didn't make me feel good. I don't really feel good
about it now. It was sick looking at all that blood and the
kid crying and it's not like I feel so bad about him because
he is a fuckhead and I hope he dies but I feel bad about
me being some badass chick who punches people because
it doesn't feel good. It feels ugly. And I kind of like it even
though I don't. I guess I like the idea of being like this girl
that nobody is going to fuck with (but not like that, ha-ha,

although I guess girls who beat the shit out of guys might not get the most dates, at least with guys but let's not get into that right now because I have enough to think about) but I don't like the jittery way I felt and I don't like the memory of the crack under my fist and I don't like the blood. Because I made him hurt doesn't make me feel better. I still feel awful. Awful.

I wonder if I will ever stop feeling awful. Sean says I will feel less awful all the time but then he cries at commercials so who the hell knows if I can believe him. Also I guess Lisa told me that I won't always feel terrible all the time and that one day I will have a day when I go a whole day without missing my moms and then I will feel guilty about it but it will keep happening because they are dead and I'm not.

Still thinking about the black album not the Metallica one but now that I am a smoker and a drunken teen and a badass chick who breaks noses of hockey players I don't know if I could stand to see something else about how I was this sweet precocious baby who was so cute. I wonder if I'll get expelled. I wonder what I would do because even with not doing the work and stuff at least school gives me something to do all day long and I can't imagine just sitting here all day with nothing to do which I guess is what Saturday and Sunday are like and which is why I will probably do some dorky bonding thing with Sean like he keeps asking me to because you can only watch so many cartoons.

I don't want to get expelled. But I don't want to go back there and have everybody talking about me and whispering and stuff and figure out how I fit in with Sasha or Jen and who wants to be friends with some violent kid.

Have I mentioned lately that I feel really bad all the time? You would think that breaking some kid's nose would help me work out my anger issues or whatever but instead it just feels like I fucked up my life even more if that is even possible just because some fuckhead kid is an asshole and it's funny to me that breaking his nose didn't even make me stop being mad at him.

>>>

To: davidsanders@Newcastle.k12.mass.edu
From: Sean_Cassidy@publaw.org
Subject: Trouble

Well, we are in some trouble here, my friend. That is to say, Rosalind is in trouble because she broke the nose of some junior hockey player (!) because he saw the same thing I TiVoed from E! about Eva dying and he was making some stupid joke about "dead dykes crushed by meat" or words to that effect.

This presents a number of problems. There are the disciplinary and legal consequences, which I am confident I can get her out of, given the fact that the hockey player in question used the word "dyke" and could reasonably be seen to be creating a hostile environment, and, in any case, mocking someone's dead parents would seem to constitute fighting words. So she is suspended from school, and we are facing an expulsion hearing, but I do, after all, sue schools for a living, and so I am feeling a great deal of confidence. And yes, I do plan to pull out that line if this meeting goes badly. I believe I told you I was saving it up for something serious, and I suppose this qualifies.

The larger problem for me (because it is, after all, all about me) is that I simply do not know how to play this as a parent. On the one hand, I don't want her to screw up her life, and she has followed the sneaking out and getting drunk with a violent assault (did I mention that she kicked him when he was down?), and I am concerned, despite your reassurances, that I am watching her become a Troubled Teen. As horrible as this is, I feel like this might be more than I signed up for. And yes, you did warn me about the difficulty of raising a teen when I made this decision, but I suppose I didn't anticipate having so many difficulties in so short a time.

Additionally, I feel that I may be partly responsible here, because I don't feel that I am handling her transgressions especially well. I simply can't help admiring her. She made us buzzword bingo cards for our first meeting with the principal. I played and won, which felt like the right thing to do at the time, because it was to some degree a bonding experience, but have I sent her the message that this doesn't matter? Is that what I'll be doing if I get her off the hook for this?

I think because I was such a goody-goody for my entire life, I really appreciate her sense of humor and willingness to be defiant. I have always had the former and lacked the latter, and I can't help looking at her and admiring her strength.

I do have to go because I am trying to prepare a rather bone-crushing defense for her in addition to filing a motion in a special-ed case that is actually what I get paid, if only nominally, to do, but I also want to say that I further admire her for breaking that kid's nose. This goes against everything I believe about violence, but I do feel like she taught that little fucker a lesson he won't soon forget, and one that he probably needed to be taught. But here, again, I am projecting my image of some hockey players from my own high school. The kid was making a cruel joke about someone he assumed was a far-off celebrity, and God knows you and I have done that enough times. Still, when she told me what he said, I wanted to punch him myself and was glad that she had done it.

I am afraid that I am allowing Rosalind to ruin her life because I am getting vicarious joy out of the things she's doing. Parenting appears to be this constant jumble of fear and guilt. Why didn't you warn me?

Yes, I know you did warn me.

—Sean

> > >

To: Sean_Cassidy@publaw.org
From: davidsanders@Newcastle.k12.mass.edu
Subject: Re: Trouble

Wow. Well, I don't have any words of wisdom about how to play it because I am glad she clocked that kid too. I would worry more about the social fallout for her, but if the kid is as much of a dick as he sounds like, kids might be carrying her on their shoulders when she gets back. Or else harassing and ostracizing her. Could go either way.

Sorry. I'm ducking your big questions because I'm fucked if I know the answers. I guess just remember that she seemed like she was fundamentally a good kid before you got her—sorry, I mean,

before her moms died, and so hopefully that good core is still
there and she will snap out of this.

I dunno, man. I got nothing here.

Why don't you guys come up here on Saturday? We'll do some
outdoorsy, fall in New England kind of stuff, or something. I haven't
seen you in too long, and maybe Rosalind could stand a little
change of scene.

Workin' for the weekend,

—D

> > >

STATEMENT OF JIM HOFFMAN
At the end of my D period English class, I was talking to
some friends when out of nowhere this girl just hit me in
the nose. She totally blindsided me, which is why I fell, and
when I fell, she kicked me. I don't know this girl. I guess I
have seen her coming into Mr. Westerberg's E period class
before, but I don't know who she is or her name or why she
hit me.

> > >

STATEMENT OF ALEX KINGMAN
It was the end of D period and the beginning of E. I have a
free period E, so I was hanging around with Jim Hoffman,
Pete Summers, and Robby Andersson, and Jim was talking
about some thing he saw on TV, and he was laughing, and
all of a sudden this girl comes up and punches him in the

face. Jim goes down, and the girl kicks him, and then Mr.
Westerberg grabbed her and Mr. Westerberg asked me to go
to the nurse, so I did.

> > >

EXPULSION HEARING OF ROSALIND BUTTERFIELD
CHARLESBOROUGH HIGH SCHOOL
Hearing Officers: Dr. Stephen Vanian, Dr. Richard Watt

SEAN CASSIDY: Before we begin, gentlemen, I would like to
    make a recording of this meeting.
STEPHEN VANIAN: Well, we write detailed minutes of the
    meetings as a matter of procedure.
SC: Then you won't have any objection to my recording this.
RICHARD WATT: No, no, that's fine, that's fine. Is that, what,
    some kind of MP3 player?
SC: Minidisc.
SV: It's like the one Scott Simon used.
RW: Right, right. All right. In any case, this hearing is now
    under way. I'd like to, if I could, piece together what I
    have from the information I've received. We have Ros-
    alind entering a classroom and consequently breaking
    Jim Hoffman's nose and kicking him—
SV: Assaulting him with a shod foot.
RW: Yes, kicking him as he lay on the ground.
SV: I need to repeat that I view this not only as an assault on
    Jim Hoffman but also as an assault upon the safe learn-
    ing environment at Charlesborough High School.
RW: As much as our instincts as educators and as human be-

ings are to be compassionate in the face of the tragedy Rosalind has undergone, it just seems that her grief has taken unacceptable forms. We have fifteen hundred students in this building, and at any given time, at least fifty of them are undergoing some sort of serious crisis. I can show you fifteen kids here who have lost parents in the last two years. So while Rosalind is not alone in this building in suffering through a difficult time, she appears to be alone when it comes to translating that difficulty into unprovoked violence. I need to tell you up front that my instinct here is to remove Rosalind from the high school and hope to find her a more appropriate placement.

SV: Mine as well.

RW: Which is not to say, again, that we do not feel compassion, and we would happily offer Rosalind access to a variety of counseling services that the town has to offer, and of course assist with a referral for an alternative placement, some kind of therapeutic setting, we have relationships with a number of programs, but I simply don't feel that Rosalind can continue here if she is going to be a threat to the safety of her classmates.

SV: As educational leaders, we have a responsibility to the entire learning community that must outweigh all other concerns.

SC: Thank you, gentlemen. Is it our turn to speak now?

RW: By all means.

SC: Fine. First of all, you've characterized this as an unprovoked assault, but I believe that characterization to be inadequate. First, according to Alex Kingman, Jim

Hoffman was telling them about something he saw on TV. If I can direct your attention to the laptop here, I actually have a clip of what Jim Hoffman was referring to, and, indeed, joking about.

Speakers: (*Music.*) And now, a sad note. We have just learned of the death last month of Eva Butterfield, who starred in commercials and made guest appearances on numerous shows in the 1970s, including *Barnaby Jones* and *Banacek*, but who was best known for her role as Tracey on *Single Dads Club*, which ran for two seasons between 1979 and '81. Long retired from acting, Eva Butterfield had become a dentist. She and her partner, Sandra Cash, were killed in a freak traffic accident near their home in the Boston area when a truckload of frozen poultry overturned.

Eva Butterfield, dead at age forty-six.

And next, bikini secrets of the stars! And, later—

SC: This is what Jim Hoffman had seen, and what he said about it, according to Rosalind, was "I was laughing my ass off, two dykes crushed by meat."

(*Silence.*)

SC: Are you gentlemen familiar with the "fighting words" doctrine?

RW: Mr. Cassidy, this isn't a court of law, and we certainly don't recognize that term in our student handbook. Part of what we try to do from the time we get kids in kindergarten is to convince them that there is no such thing as fighting words.

SC: Fair enough. I do want to point out, however, that there is a long legal history to the idea that some kinds of speech are inherently so provocative that they might cause a reasonable person to act violently. Surely someone mocking the death of one's parents qualifies here.

RW: I'll admit that this does place a slightly different spin on the incident, but only slightly. She did not attempt to resolve the situation verbally at all. Honestly, if she had just sworn at him, that would be against the rules, but that would have meant a "tut-tut" in the counselor's office, and we wouldn't be sitting here today. The fact is that Rosalind went directly to violence with no intervening steps. I understand what you are saying about what Jim said, I do, but this was not any kind of intentional mockery on his part. He doesn't even know Rosalind.

SC: I dare say he knows her now, but whether this is intentional or not on his part is, for the moment, beside the point. My point, which I think you will concede, is that this was not an unprovoked act of violence, but rather an extreme but not pathological response to provocative language. I will grant you that Rosalind should have reacted differently and that her use of violence here was inappropriate, which is why we aren't appealing the suspension. But this is just not an expulsion offense.

(*Silence.*)

RW: All right. I will grant you that knowing that Jim Hoffman was making a joke about this does change the character of the incident. Provided, of course, that we can verify that, it does change the character of the incident.

SC: Actually, Dr. Watt, it changes the character of the incident quite considerably. For, indeed, Jim Hoffman, with his use of the word *dyke,* appears to me to be creating a hostile environment for lesbian students as well as, in this case, family members of lesbians.

SV: Well, Mr. Cassidy, I think we all know that the average teenager is not always a paragon of sensitivity.

SC: Which is neither here nor there. Chapter 76, Section 5 of Massachusetts General Law, with which you are no doubt familiar, states, and I quote: "No person shall be excluded from or discriminated against in admission to a public school of any town or"—and here is the relevant part for this matter—"in obtaining the advantages, privileges, and courses of study of such public school on account of race, color, sex, religion, national origin, or sexual orientation."

Now, it seems to me that Rosalind being unable to walk into a classroom without hearing degrading, dehumanizing, and harassing language about her family constitutes her being discriminated against in obtaining the advantages and courses of study of this public school.

SV: Realistically, Mr. Cassidy, we can't control everything that comes out of every student's mouth.

SC: No, but you have a responsibility to provide and maintain an atmosphere that is not hostile. What have you done to raise your students' awareness of this issue?

SV: Well, our harassment policy appears in the student handbook, which every student receives a copy of.

SC: How many students have you suspended for hate speech against gays and lesbians in the last five years?

RW: Well, obviously that's not a number we have at our fingertips.

SC: Indeed, but you will if I take this to court, and if I had to guess, I'd put that number at zero. I would remind you gentlemen that I sue schools for a living, and if Rosalind is expelled for this I will sue under Chapter 76, Section 5 as well as any other relevant statutes I can find. I am sure Lambda Legal Defense would love to help me out on this case, and I am further sure that a great deal of negative publicity would accrue to your district as a result.

SV: But she punched Jim Hoffman in the face! She broke his nose!

SC: And, in accordance with the rules set out in your handbook, she's been suspended, which we feel is fair.

RW: Fine, Mr. Cassidy, we'll meet in private and inform you of our decision when we're done.

(*Sounds of shuffling, chairs moving, walking.*)

ROSALIND BUTTERFIELD: So, uh, thanks.

SC: Well, you're welcome.

RB: You know, as soon as Vanian said "learning community," I just thought, "Bingo!"

SC: Well, it's hardly fair if you don't make a card for me. But I am really really glad you didn't say that in the meeting.

RB: Yeah, next time I'm gonna make one *about* you. How many times did you say "hostile environment"?

SC: I don't know. I was shooting for five. It's in the definition of "harassment."

RB: Yeah, I got that actually. I liked "accrue" too. "Bad publicity will accrue."

SC: Um, Rosalind?

RB: Yeah?

SC: I would really really—I mean, I don't think I can really add enough reallys here to make clear how much I would like this, but I would really—

RB: Times double infinity plus one?

SC: Yeah, really times double infinity plus one like it if we didn't have a next time.

RB: (*Pause.*) Me too.

SC: (*Pause.*) How do you rate our chances of that?

RB: I dunno. I guess I wouldn't have said I thought this one was ever gonna happen. I mean, if you asked me if I was going to break some kid's nose, I would have said no way, but then I did. So I don't think it'll happen again, and I actually don't want it to happen again, and I guess that's about the best I can do for you.

SC: I'll take it. (*Pause.*) Hungry?

RB: I'm starving.

SC: How about that Chinese place with the gluten mock duck and whatever.

RB: Okay. Hey, are you still recording?

SC: No, I'm pretty sure—

RB: No, look, the light's on. No wonder your damn batteries run out all the time, you

END

> > >

Dear Fluffy:

Well, Sean got me off the hook, off the heezie for sheezie, whatever, I am not getting expelled. Which is good I guess except it means I have to go back to school. I'm kind of scared about what people are going to say. Maybe I should call Sasha and see what people are saying.

So I guess I am going with Sean to his dorky gym teacher friend's house to do some kind of fake family bonding or whatever. I mean the bonding is fake because I don't want to and the family is fake because of obvious reasons.

I kind of wonder if I should start doing work or something at school, I am kind of ready for something to go right, to not be like screwed up about everything, but I'm still really sad and I can't make myself believe it's important anymore. I'd like to feel good about something. I mean, I guess I felt good about getting drunk, but I can't do that every day, I mean I could probably but then I would be like that guy on Centre Street with the 40 in a paper bag yelling at people and that would be okay I guess, but I don't see it as something I would be into for a long time, but then again that guy has been at it as long as I can remember so maybe it has possibilities as a long-term career. But I guess he has dibs on that spot.

OK, now I get drunk, break noses and make fun of homeless guys, and also smoke, and maybe I will kick a puppy. I kind of wonder if Mom and Mommy would recognize me and if they would like me or if they would be all "We're so disappointed in you." Well, too bad, I guess, I mean maybe I could be my old self if they were here to make me feel guilty about my new self but of course the new self is only because they're not here and I guess that's another conundrum or logic puzzle or something. In the movies there is always somebody saying, "Oh, the spirit of my father is guiding me" or something, I think that was actually in that Mount Everest movie, but I don't feel them at all, I don't feel like they are smiling at me from heaven or anything, all I feel is space where they used to be. I would like a little smile from heaven, a little Mufasa face in the clouds saying Ros do your homework it's important or something, but oh well life is not like cartoons because if it was maybe that kid's nose would have just spun around his head a couple times instead of cracking like that.

I'm tired. I want to have fun again. I want something to be fun. But then I guess like Lisa said then I would feel guilty about not feeling sad and it is pretty great to be me right now except I guess at least I do have this bed to fall into which is what I am doing now goodbye.

> > >

To: Rosalind90@aol.com
From: Sean_Cassidy@publaw.org
Subject: what happens next

Rosalind,

I thought I would tell you something about myself again. I am feeling a very strong urge to do or say something relating to your hearing, but I am going to restrain myself. I appreciate the fact that you don't want this to happen again, and I would like to help you if I can. Unfortunately, I don't know what to do to help. I thought I might try to say the words "hostile environment" a bunch of times, or possibly "not complying with his IEP" (that is a special-ed joke) (that is to say, a joke about special-education regulations, not a special-ed joke like "Dave's a sped").

I am babbling because I want to say something to you but I don't know what it is. So I thought I would tell you something about what happened to me after my mother died. I suppose my career choice makes it relatively obvious that I decided at age ten that I should become her. I suppose my thought process was that our family was a one-bartender, one-lawyer unit and we were now short a lawyer, so I had to start studying so that I could be a good lawyer and make my mother proud.

So I hit the books, pretty much to the exclusion of all else. There are only so many books you can hit in the fifth grade, so I actually went after school and asked for extra sets of math problems, extra reading books, anything that would help me to study.

I suppose if this were a movie, sometime in high school I would have eventually realized that studying could not take the place of my mother, and that I needed to be more well-rounded and get a date or a life, but, of course, this isn't a movie, which I suppose is why my mother never looked down at me, Mufasa-like, and told me I was a good lawyer and she was proud of me. That is a *Lion King* joke, which I am almost certain you get because according to my friend Dave, that movie is now an initiation rite of American childhood.

I watched it with his son Max once. Of course I cried at the end, and I hated the whole thing for any number of reasons, not least of which was the political implications. I would have liked Simba to

declare the monarchy obsolete and found a republic, but that, I
suppose, is what came of too much extra reading in history. And,
ultimately, I suppose the Lion Prime Minister doesn't sound quite
as good.

Mostly, though, I hated it because of that lie at the end that
Mufasa is going to smile at you if you make him proud. The fact is
that I have spent the last twenty-six years trying to make my
mother proud, and though I continue to look to the clouds, I never
see her face. I don't know if she's proud of me, or if she continues
to exist in any way, or if she does if she is even aware of me. Many
people seem to be sure about this, and I envy their certainty.
They say things like, "She's always with you" and "I just know your
mother's proud of you" (those are from cards I got from my aunts
when I passed the bar). I don't know. I have never felt it since the
day she died, that certainty of her presence that I always took for
granted before then.

I am not sure in the end why I am telling you this. I don't feel
like I am someone you should emulate in my path out of grief, so
this is not some veiled lecture about why you should hit the books,
because ultimately my book hitting did not bring my mom back or
get me one benevolent gaze from the clouds. I don't know if real
parents, ones who don't just appear after fourteen years, are better at shaping their anecdotes into little life lessons. I don't know
what my story should mean to you, if anything. Let me know if you
figure anything out.

—Sean

> > >

To: Sean_Cassidy@publaw.org
From: Rosalind90@aol.com
Subject: Re: what happens next

Nothing yet. I will let you know.

—R

> > >

IM from Sashutup

Sashutup: HOWRU? RU XPLED?
Rosalind90: HEY. NT XPLED!
Sashutup: IM GLAD
Rosalind90: ME2.
Sashutup: PEOPLE R TALKING ABOUT U
Rosalind90: FUCKEM. BUT WHAT R THEY SAYIN?
Sashutup: UVE LOST IT SYCO, BLAH BLAH
Rosalind90: FUCKEM AGAIN. I LOST IT BUT IM NOT SYCO ☺
Sashutup: I TOLD JENNYM THAT ID BREAK HER NOSE 2 IF SHE DIDNT SHUTUP. ☺
Rosalind90: URA TRU FRND. BUT JENNYM MIGHT LIKE A BROKN NOSE CUZ SHE COULD GET THE NOSE JOB SHE NEEDS SO BAD.
Sashutup: ☺
Sashutup: I MISS U. WANNA COME OVER?
Rosalind90: YEAH BUT I PROMISED DONORBOY TO DO SOME DORKY HIKNG OR SOMETHING. ☹ NEXT WKND?
Sashutup: OK. IL ASK MOM. CU
Rosalind90: CU!

> > >

To: Sean_Cassidy@publaw.org
From: davidsanders@Newcastle.k12.mass.edu
Subject: Thanks for coming up

Hey there. I just wanted to say thanks for coming up and how much I enjoyed meeting Rosalind. Not that she said two words to me, but Max is apparently deeply in love with her. Ever since you left he's been asking when Sean and Rosalind are coming again, can we go down and see Sean and Rosalind, maybe Sean and Rosalind can come for Thanksgiving, etc. So she made quite an impression on him. Hopefully she didn't teach him to smoke or anything. That's a joke. So do you think the trip accomplished the bonding you had hoped? Or was it just a walk on the beach? In any case, it was great to see you. Let's not wait so long next time.

> > >

To: davidsanders@Newcastle.k12.mass.edu
From: Sean_Cassidy@publaw.org
Subject: Re: Thanks for coming up

Well, I am not certain if the requisite bonding was accomplished or not. That is to say, we did actually talk in the car, at least on the way up, mostly so she could criticize the music I was playing, though we seem to have found some common ground in the Donnas. Though this too caused me to get all uptight about my parenting failure. Should I be commenting that I don't think a song like "Take Me to the Backseat" really expresses a healthy attitude toward sexuality? Should I tell her that female empowerment doesn't necessarily mean hard-partying sleaze? Or should I just roll the windows down and turn the volume up?

Guess which option I chose.

She was silent and sullen all the way home. You would be very proud of me—I managed not to ask her what she was thinking, or how she was doing, or anything. So I suppose that was a positive, though of course when I fail to get in her face I worry that I am being the kind of father my dad was. Ah, that exquisite fear and guilt mélange again.

In any case, it wasn't horrible, she spoke for half the trip, she hung out with Max without punching him, so I suppose we have to count it as a success. I also enjoyed it a lot. Not to feed poor Max's unrequited love too much, but perhaps the three of you could come down here for dinner or something sometime.

Well, back to work. Having brought Charlesborough to heel, I now have to take on some charter school that thinks they don't have to do special ed. Talk to you soon,

—Sean

> > >

Dear Fluffy:

Corny bonding day with Sean and his dorky friend was okay, I guess, but why do gym teachers always have those gigantic guts? I seriously can't believe that guy teaches gym. And his wife is this good-looking woman just like on commercials where some fat bonehead always has a pretty wife. Well, the world is weird I guess.

His kid was okay. I beat him at Smash Brothers, so I think he thinks I am a goddess which of course I am, ha ha. I got sad at the beach though. Because the great sea is a metaphor for my own tiny insignificance. Ha, no, but maybe if I made some bullshit poem out of that Westerberg would give me extra credit. It just made me miss going to P-town every summer and the beaches there and the sea is still there but Mom and Mommy are gone, and I don't know I guess I thought maybe they took all the beaches with them or something. Plus I probably will never go to P-town with Sean because I just don't think single straight guys go there unless like their gay dad has a house there or something. Anyway who wants to go there without Mom and Mommy anyway.

So I was quiet for a while and I was glad Sean didn't try to talk to me or bring up something serious like "Oh, I notice you are quiet, and so I'd like to talk about why you are failing everything, or maybe you need to open up, or I'm here for you" but luckily like I said he just shut up and played his old-school dork music.

So tomorrow is back to school and it's 11:30 and I am nervous about walking into class again and everything and I wonder if that kid's friends will be mean to me or what. Probably I will start going like five minutes late to Westerberg's class so I can just not see that fuckhead and his fuckhead friends, but then I will be making this big entrance into English class which is not good either. Ladies and Gentlemen, Rosalind the psycho has arrived! Watch your mouth, or she'll rearrange your face! Blah blah blah.

Guess I should go to bed but I don't want to because when
I go to bed it will make it almost tomorrow but if I stay up
it will still be today. Whatever. I am tired of you tonight
Fluffy, no offense or anything but maybe I will watch TV.

> > >

Dear Fluffy:
Well, school wasn't that bad because as I suspected people
are kind of afraid of me and that is cool and I do think the
BWP were being extra friendly or respectful or something
but maybe I am imagining that. Anyway Jen welcomed
me back personally in the hallway, all "I heard that kid
made fun of your moms and I'm glad you flattened him,"
and so did Kate the Shoplifter, only I should stop calling
her that because she has always only been nice to me and
so I shouldn't be a bitch and make fun of her even though
I'm sorry but she could boost some nice stuff and not just
metal shirts. Okay that was mean and from now on I am
never making fun of Kate again because like I said she is
only ever nice to me and that counts for a lot especially
when half of the school is looking at me like I am the psycho bitch from hell.

So, whatever, dorks look at me like they are afraid
of me and I don't care even though it does kind of seem
funny if you think that at the end of last year I was the
last person anybody would ever be afraid of, just another
plain flat-chested girl with a headband and way too many
freckles, and now I am some badass but I guess I need a

Metallica shirt or a Red Chord shirt or whatever Kate is always wearing. I don't think that counts as making fun of her because it's just what she wears.

I did hate lunch though and I don't know what to do about lunch because I do want to be friends with the BWP and also Sasha and Kristen and Sara, well, Sasha and Kristen anyway, I swear to God I am going to kill Sara if she doesn't shut up about how she hates her mom, stupid ungrateful bitch.

So where do I sit at lunchtime, because wherever I sit it's like I am rejecting somebody, so today I just hid in the bathroom and smoked and Jen wasn't there for some reason and nobody else came in except for some skinny girl who looks about twelve who looked really afraid of me which I kind of liked. So that was okay I guess as a solution to the which table problem, except that I was lonely and I didn't get to eat but if you smoke enough you don't really miss the food but it does make you smell.

I guess it's good that I care about hurting people's feelings now, because I actually care about something, which is something that hasn't happened in a while, but mostly it's not that so much as I am just tired of being the alone sad girl and so I don't want to piss anybody off by choosing somebody else because then I'll be the alone sad girl again instead of just the sad girl which I always am anyway, but the only way not to piss people off is to be the alone sad girl. Which counts as a conundrum I guess.

Fuck this anyway. I am too tired to worry about this shit, but then I guess I'm not because my stomach is getting all knotty just thinking about it oh well.

>>>

IM from Sashutup

Sashutup: HELLO?

Rosalind90: HELLO. HOW RU?

Sashutup: GOOD BUT IM SORRY BUT I JUST WONDER WHY U DIDN'T SIT W/US TODAY.

Rosalind90: I DON'T KNOW, I DON'T KNOW I GUESS I JUST WANTED TO TALK TO JEN TODAY

Sashutup: RU STILL MY BF?

Rosalind90: YES. I JUST FELT LIKE SITTING THERE TODAY. SOME-TIMES WHEN IM SAD I LIKE TO SIT WITH THEM B/C THEY R SAD 2.

Sashutup: WELL I AM THERE 4U

Rosalind90: I KNOW, I JUST WANTED TO SIT OVER THERE TODAY. IM STILL COMING OVER SAT ANYWAY IF IM STILL INVITED

Sashutup: OF COURSE UR.

Rosalind90: OK I AM TIRED SO BYE

Sashutup: RU MAD AT ME?

Rosalind90: IM JUST TIRED. GOODNITE.

>>>

Dear Fluffy:

I swear to God Sasha is a pain in my ass. "Are you still my BF?" This is why I hate lunch now because today I was smoking with Jen and then she said come on in and have lunch and what am I going to say, no I am afraid that Sasha might be jealous and thinking of somebody who should be afraid they are a lesbian maybe it's not me because it's not like I am her girlfriend or something but she acts like it.

What am I going to do? Where I am I going to eat? I fucking hate this stupid shit. fuck fuck fuck. If I have to pick maybe I will pick my nose ha ha. No but what I was going to say is that Jen and Kate never ask me why I didn't want to sit with them if I sit with Sasha and I don't know if it's because they are just more real or if they don't care because they don't like me as much. Maybe I will sit by myself and see who sits with me. Who cares anyway I guess if somebody is going to disown me over lunch then fuck them, but on the other hand it's not like I have so many friends that I can afford to lose any, especially since my family is now short one teacher and one dentist as Sean might say and I am sorry Mom but I think I would kill myself if I had to do either one of those things and like Sean says you are not going to look down and smile at me so maybe that is what his story means, that you just have to do whatever because somebody who is dead can't be proud of you.

That sounds kind of harsh. I am sorry Mom, but I guess it is true, except if I am talking to you then I guess I don't really believe it because it sounds too harsh to say you are dead even if you are dead and it feels harsh too and I still think you're going to be mad at me for saying you can't be proud of me and this is another conundrum I guess.

I don't know anything. I am not worrying about lunch anymore because if I can't please my moms I don't give a shit about pleasing Sasha or Kate or whoever. I am going to smoke my cigarette and eat wherever I feel like and I am not making a schedule even though I did start doing that in my notebook trying to be like how can I sit at both tables equally like week A it's three days and week B it's two days or something and how dumb is that that I actually started drawing this thing but that is just too dumb. I am sitting where I feel like and they can get over it.

> > >

MINIDISC #72: RECORDED 11/13/04.

Good evening, or should I say good morning. I am talking into the minidisc recorder just like Scott Simon from NPR uses because I don't know who else to talk to. Dave would say he didn't mind, but I hate to be the wussy pal who calls in the middle of the night, so I am going to try to get through this particular crisis with just me and the recorder. Just to bring you up to speed, I just got a call from Mrs. or possibly Ms. Cervenka, who by the way sounds very cute on the phone, asking me if Rosalind and Sasha were here because she just checked on them and found them missing.

It is now one a.m. I don't know where my child is. I am vacillating between anger and terror, and right now anger seems to have the upper hand. Why is she doing this to me? I mean, I certainly try, I bought all the burritos, I stuck up for her in meetings, and I feel like I get this kind of kick in the teeth in response.

Shit!

(Thumping sounds.)

That series of thumps, by the way, was the sound of me

punching the couch. It was quite unsatisfying and made me feel silly.

I am going to die if anything happens to her. I will kill myself if Karen and possibly Ros's grandmother and uncle Mike don't do it for me. I suspect she is probably fine, probably at some party again, and I'd really like to go out and drive around walking distance from Sasha's house looking for parties, but then if she came here, she . . . but of course it is Sasha's house they are going to be sneaking into.

Can I really go haul her out of a party? Didn't someone's father do that in *Weird Science*? or *Sixteen Candles*? Some John Hughes movie, anyway. I suppose that would make her a social pariah, with the popular kids pointing and laughing and eventually electing her prom queen and dumping pig blood on her.

Then again, I do recall about eight years ago that a girl died of alcohol poisoning while the other partygoers stepped over her at a party like this.

Then again, most kids who go to parties don't end up dead, they just end up drunk.

All right, I can't just sit here waiting for the phone to ring. I am getting in the car.

STOP.

Okay, I am here in the car and I feel like some kind of deranged stalker. Perhaps that is what fatherhood is all about. So far it seems to be about sleeping poorly on the weekends and worrying a great deal. I am not sure I am cut out for it.

In any case, I am sitting here in my car listening to my Pixies mix for the hundredth time and watching the teens exit the party, which I did locate with very little difficulty and which I cannot understand why Charlesborough police are allowing to continue. Especially since I phoned in a noise complaint. In any case, I am hoping to nab her as she exits. I suppose this is my compromise, that I will only embarrass her in front of her friend instead of the whole school.

I have no idea if I am doing the right thing, or if I am overreacting, but I am starting to feel actually physically sick from anxiety. It appears to be similar to drinking a quadruple espresso. Except it tastes much less like coffee and more like bile. I am jittery and my heart is pounding and my stomach feels sour.

I am going to . . . okay, there she is. Bye.

> > >

Dear Fluffy:
I think I am under house arrest. Anyway Sean is wicked mad (I wonder if I could say "mad mad" but that sounds dumb so maybe mad angry or mad heated) because Sasha's mom decided to check on us and I swear to God I feel like we are the only two people on earth whose parents don't like completely ignore them as soon as they shut their door. But anyway, we snuck out to a party that some guy from Sasha's math class was having, or anyway him and his older brother, and there were a ton of people there and ironically enough it was actually not fun, and I don't know if that is like dramatic irony or situational irony or whatever kinds of irony Westerberg thinks we should

know about, but anyway I am in deep shit because I went to a party that wasn't fun because I guess I got too drunk too fast or something but instead of forgetting about being sad like last time I actually got more sad, and I kept drinking to make it go away but it just got worse, and so I am there on the lawn crying with Sasha hugging me and it was embarrassing because now I am the girl who punched a kid and makes a scene at a party, all crying can't handle her booze whatever. Probably everybody will be convinced I am a psycho now, but I guess maybe they were already. So as soon as I could talk I was like I want to go home and we walk out and there was Sean the stalker all "get in the car" and driving us home and not saying anything and turning the music off until we dropped Sasha off.

And then he totally starts yelling at me, really like I have never seen him before, all he was worried sick "literally sick, Rosalind!" which sounded kind of funny and maybe I will put that on a bingo card for next time, but anyway, I was like whatever, what's the big deal and he was like because alcohol can make you make bad decisions, all There are boys there who want to get you drunk and blah blah.

I was totally like that is your heterosexist bias how do you even know that I care if boys are hitting on me and that shut him up for a while but then he was all quiet like, "I guess that's not really the issue. It's just that I care about you and I don't know what to do if I can't trust you."

Boo hoo, poor guy, but I don't really care, except I just wrote it down so maybe I do, so now whatever I am bad

again and I make people mad and sad and I was glad he
didn't call Karen again, but you know he's going to tell her
and then I will have to hear it from her, all what are you
doing and what I am doing is just trying to not feel sad for
five minutes because I am so tired of always being sad,
and I thought being drunk would help me be not sad, and
I know Westerberg it is a cruel irony that it didn't work is
what kind of irony it is. Anyway, I just want to feel good
like normal kids, like all those Abercrombie kids who
walked around me all laughing and holding their red plastic cups. Which I guess I am wearing Abercrombie too so
shut up. I don't get why they get to have fun and I have to
sit on the grass and cry, all I want to do is feel good and I
guess I don't think that is so terrible but I guess I am all
alone on this one.

> > >

To: davidsanders@Newcastle.k12.mass.edu
From: Sean_Cassidy@publaw.org
Subject: Party all the time

Yes, as in my girl wants to.

    I just don't know what the hell I am supposed to do here. I am
completely at a loss. Rosalind sneaked out again, this time from
her friend Sasha's house. I got a species of angry I don't believe I
have ever gotten before. I went slightly insane. Or else I was a wonderful parent. In any case, I figured if the party was big, it would
not be that difficult to locate, so I drove around in about a mile ra-

dius from her friend's house until I located said party and then monitored the exits because, as angry as I was, I still did not want to humiliate her by dragging her out of the party.

Actually, that's only partially true. I also, at age thirty-five, did not want a house full of drunken fifteen-year-olds to be looking at me as a dorky, overprotective father. Don't ask me why my image with a bunch of half-soused hormone-crazed teens is important to me, as I do not have an answer. Thankfully she did not die of alcohol poisoning or get date-raped by some curvy-baseball-cap wearing, Korn-listening senior boy. If either of those things had happened, then I would have had a lifetime to examine my mixed motives for not entering the actual party. As it was, I nabbed her and her friend on their exit from the party and returned her friend to her house. (A depressing side note to this little adventure is that said friend's mother sounds very attractive on the phone, and I was mindful of your comment about single moms on the playground, so I was very disappointed upon my arrival to find that she is, shall we say, somewhat less than very attractive in person. Actually she is far less than very attractive. I believe the colloquial term is "fugly.")

Once her friend was safely out of the car, I yelled at Rosalind like I never had before, and she dug in her heels and told me I was a heterosexist for assuming that she would care about guys hitting on her. This brought me up short. (I decided that she may have been right, and also that I have no idea if there are predatory, curvy-baseball-cap wearing, Korn . . . no—I don't know, is there an angry lesbian metal band? Is this a market niche?—lesbian senior girls who try to get fourteen-year-old girls drunk at house parties and take advantage of them. I have no evidence, but I strongly suspect this is not the case.) But I ultimately told her that the prob-

lem was that I care so much about her and hate that I can't trust
her. I did not bother explaining how I care so much that I am literally having panic attacks—sweat, palpitations, shortness of
breath—when I don't know what's happening to her. This sucks, my
friend. I am once again questioning the wisdom of my decision
here. Not only because I don't appear to be doing very well by her,
but because becoming a father in a real sense has not brought me
the kind of fulfillment I had hoped it would. It seems that in the
normal course of events, you have children and they are these cute
little bundles of joy for several years and you bank that joy against
the time when they will be pain-in-the-ass teenagers who will
break your heart. And I have so very little joy in the bank. Just
more heartbreak.

All right, that sounded maudlin even to me. In any event, Rosalind is grounded until the next millennium, though I can't imagine
that is going to stop her if she is determined to misbehave.

I am sad. Encourage me.

—Sean

> > >

To: Sean_Cassidy@publaw.org
From: davidsanders@Newcastle.k12.mass.edu
Subject: Re: Party all the time

Sean—
You are right. That was maudlin. And let me correct your miscon-
ception here. Babies are cute little bundles of joy, and you bank
that joy against the time when they are screaming for no reason

at three a.m., puking on you, and covering you in liquid shit. Also, as they age, throwing things, saying they hate you, and having a seemingly unerring instinct to stomp your nuts. Well, maybe that last part is just Max, who, at age six, keeps giving me shots to the nads that I think might not always be accidental. Anyway, it's always joy and pain like sunshine and rain or whatever that crappy song was, and no, Mr. Rock Critic, I do not want to hear about what you think of the songs I don't consider crappy.

I'm sorry this is so hard. I hate to say I told you so—okay, that is a total lie. I hate to see you sad, but the upside for me is that I get to say I told you so. I told you it was going to be hard in ways you couldn't imagine, and you said you didn't care, that this was the right thing to do, that this is what you wanted to do, that it didn't matter if it was hard, because it needed to be done. That was a good argument. It convinced me. But that might just be that I am a gym teacher in the sticks and am easily swayed by your fast-talkin' big city lawyerin' ways. Don't give up, and please go see a doctor about the panic attacks.

—Dave

> > >

Dear Fluffy:
Well, house arrest is kind of a joke, I mean to say it's like I get full Fluffy access but I have to hand over my phone when I get home and I once again don't have any IM access. But I don't know, Fluffy, if I really want to talk to anybody that bad anyway. Mostly when I get home or whatever you want to call this place, Sean's apartment, my

apartment, my place where I live with my donor, I just start feeling sad and I just want to read and maybe talk to you Fluffy, and I just don't want to talk to anybody from school because I can just about convince myself that school is not completely ridiculous when I'm there but once I'm home it's like who cares.

But anyway house arrest is also a joke because school gets out at 2:42 and Sean gets home at 6, and I guess that's why 4:20 is so popular, though it's not popular around here like that.

But anyway today something kind of good happened which is that Jen and Kate and Terri who is another bitch with problems even though she seems really nice and I don't know what her problem is but anyway they go to this gross diner I never even noticed before for coffee after school every day, and today they asked me and at first I was like well I am grounded but then I was like well I can be home by 5 and still not have the warden find out, so that is cool. I liked it there because there were just diner people there and not Starbucks people, and so I didn't miss Mom or Mommy there because we never used to be diner people, we were definitely Starbucks people, vente hot chocolate for me please, no not thinking that not thinking about it anyway I drank coffee which probably is making my breath fresh as a summer breeze douche or something when you combine it with the cigarettes, but we just sat there and I mostly listened while they talked about music and guys and stuff and one thing that was kind of funny is that they sounded like Sasha or Kristen or somebody except that they were talking about guys who I guess were way older and not even in high school and probably not in college either and yeah I still find that kinda scary. Which is kind of sad I guess, but whatever. I mean, it's not sad, I guess it feels okay to be scared of hanging out with guys that old because then you totally end up on Jerry Springer having Steve hold your kid while you try to scratch your best friend's eyes out for stealing your man or something.

Is that mean? I don't know. I mean, I wouldn't want to see any of them on Jerry Springer or anything, but it's not like I am a good enough friend to be like maybe the 25-year-old guy who works in the record store might not be your best boyfriend choice.

And what about me? Was I jealous when Jen was talking about whatever boy she likes? I don't think so. Actually Jen is kind of starting to bum me out and I actually like Kate a little better. She is always sketching and she draws pretty fucked up stuff like skulls and horror movie stuff or metal album covers or something, but maybe drawing all that horrible stuff makes her happier in person because Jen is always bummed out which like I say I do like sometimes when I am bummed because then we can be bummed together but sometimes I would rather have a distraction. Anyway, I wish I could draw skulls or something because I would like to have something that made me happy right now or at least some place to put the sad.

Still failing but I did almost care when everybody was staying after to check their grades and I was like why bother. I am not an artist. I am not a shoplifter. I am not a goody goody going to Harvard early decision, not with

these grades missy. I am not a druggy. I am nothing, I am
just me, just Rosalind, just a block of sad with a girl
around it.

> > >

To: Sean_Cassidy@publaw.org
From: Rosalind90@aol.com
Subject: it didn't work

I just thought you might like to know which you didn't seem to
notice because you were yelling at me so much but I did actually
spend most of my time at that party crying. Which I am not plead-
ing for leniency or anything your honor, but I just thought I would
tell you that it wasn't fun, so it's not like there is too much danger
of me doing it again. I thought it would make me feel better and it
made me feel actually worse.

Is this ever going to stop? How long before you had fun again?

> > >

To: Rosalind90@aol.com
From: Sean_Cassidy@publaw.org
Subject: Re: it didn't work

Rosalind—Thank you for writing. I really do appreciate it, and I
suppose I must cop to your implicit criticism that I was more concerned with reading you the riot act than with whatever might
have been happening to you at the time. Which apparently was a

Weepy Drunk, which I am sorry to inform you is a Cassidy family tradition. (You do not bear the name, but you do bear the DNA, which I am afraid is where the Weepy Drunk gene resides.)

I have not forgotten your question. Bear with me.

It was not uncommon for my father to spend his off-nights getting plowed and then weeping about how much he missed Mom, what a bad father he was to me, he was sorry but he was a mess. I am not certain if he noticed when I stopped disagreeing with him.

But I digress. I, myself, had my alcohol experimentation, primarily in college, and I too found that on some occasions it made me feel good, while on others I would spend the entire evening crying into my red plastic cup full of foamy Milwaukee's Best because I wanted my mommy. So if you have learned that booze is a treacherous friend, you are well ahead of me. I believe I was twenty-two and a year out of college before I decided that I really couldn't trust drinking to excess, because the crying was even worse than the hangover.

As for when I had fun again—well, remember that I was nine years old. And *Star Wars* came out the previous summer. So I was one of these kids you may have heard or read about who saw the movie weekly for about a year and a half, and I used to be able to play Star Wars with my friends (almost inevitably getting stuck with the loser role of Wedge. Too shy for Luke, too wimpy for Han, too small for Chewbacca. I did score Obi-Wan a few times . . . but I digress.)

So, in some respects, I was able to have fun almost immediately, in the way that children can. And then I would cry in the evenings.

I put the crying away after a few months—honestly I don't remember—more than two, but fewer than six. And, as I said, I studied, which helped.

And then once I got into Penn (where I didn't really want to go and obviously didn't, but I applied as a sort of tribute to my mother), that is to say as I held the acceptance letter in my hand, it was like the dam burst, and I cried for what seemed like hours. Actually, I know for a fact that it was at least an hour because I happened to be watching a rerun of *The Big Valley* when the mail came, and when I looked up from crying, Channel Six news was almost over.

After that, I was more keenly aware of the sadness, and it bubbled up very frequently in college. See "Weepy Drunk," above.

I suppose this is just a variation of what I told you before. All I can say is that it will get better. "Of course, she is sometimes a big pain in my butt, as I guess kids her age are supposed to be, but I am amazed to see this wonderful, strong woman peeking out from behind my little girl. I see her becoming the woman I still wish I could be. I am so proud of her."

I can't offer you Mufasa, but that is what Eva wrote about you on your fourteenth birthday. Apologies if you've already been through the photo album and read it, and apologies too if it made you cry. I just want to encourage you, and I thought she said it better than I could.

Love,
Sean

> > >

To: Sean_Cassidy@publaw.org
From: Rosalind90@aol.com
Subject: Re: Re: it didn't work

It did make me cry but thank you all the same.

—R

      > > >

Dear Fluffy:
Sean made me cry with his stupid nice e-mail, and the thing that made me really mad or sad or something was that I couldn't talk back. I mean, Mom says this nice thing about me, or anyway Sean tells me what it is and then I want to say, that's great, but I could use a little help here because I don't know how to do this, I don't know how to be this orphan kid, it's a hard knock life.

I thought maybe going to the cemetery would help since I haven't been there since it happened and anyway in the movies and on tv, that's where people always go to talk to their dead relatives, all, "well, Dad, I finally caught your killer so rest in peace."

Kate asked me if I was going to the diner and I guess I wanted some sympathy or something so I was like no I am going to the cemetery to see my moms' graves, and she was like can I go with you and I thought that was pretty nice. I kind of think that she thinks the cemetery is a kind of metal place to go and maybe she can get some

good death metal art ideas, but whatever, I don't have to
go by myself, even though I kind of wanted to go by myself because if you are being a dork and talking to the air,
all "Mom help me out here," it helps to not have somebody there looking at you like you're a psycho, but maybe
Kate wouldn't do that, but anyway I wasn't exactly super
comfortable having a weepy heart to heart in front of her
(not even a weepy drunk, ha ha though even now I probably wouldn't say no because what the hell, so far there is
only a 50-50 chance I'm going to cry when I'm drinking
which is actually a lot better odds than real life). But anyway we took the T to Forest Hills which by the way is not
actually that close to Forest Hills Cemetery, we had to
walk for like fifteen minutes but whatever, and once we
got there it was a total mess and I wandered around looking for their gravestones because I remember where it
was sort of but not really, so I got totally lost walking
around all the dead people. Finally we found it and Kate
without me even having to ask or anything said I'm
gonna go sketch back there by the pond you can come and
find me when you're done, and I thought that was pretty
cool because I didn't know how to ask her to buzz off but
then she did.

So I stood there for a while all "hello?" and not like I
expected an answer or anything though that might have
been nice, but really I just wanted to see if I felt any different, like they were listening to me or something. I
didn't feel anything, and that made me sad, and so finally
I was crying and I was just like I don't know if you can

hear me but I need some help because this is really really hard and I know you didn't want to die but I'm kinda fucked up here and I need you to help me.

I don't know if they heard me or not, but they sure as hell didn't say anything. So that made me sad and I was crying and oh I forgot to mention that there were flowers on each of their graves which I thought was pretty nice of Karen to do because I guess I have been neglecting them or whatever but I didn't think they were there and I thought being there would remind me of when they died and it did so I don't think I'll be going back too soon.

Walking back to find Kate I saw outside the fence that there was the DYS lockup like right there next to the cemetery which is I guess where I would have gone if I had ever gotten arrested for the shod foot incident which I don't really know why I didn't except that maybe this hockey player kid was embarrassed that I cleaned his clock which I feel kind of proud of which I am ashamed of.

Anyway so the juvenile jail is right there next to where their graves are and I wondered if I could see their graves if I was there and isn't that an example of dramatic irony or one of the other kinds, or maybe it's like my situation writ large which is a good phrase, but anyway writ large in the geography of Boston, the big cemetery next to the big lockup because the one would lead right to the other, they ought to make a door in the fence or something.

I found Kate and she was sketching this girl who was in a glass cage, I mean it was a statue of the girl and she was all dressed up and Kate was like she was four and how fucked up is that, and I was like yeah, and it's too bad she's in that cage and it was funny because I really did feel bad for her, like she was really there in a cage even though it was just a hunk of rock in the shape of a girl, and now I'm like well how weird is that that I think I can feel this kid here but not my own moms.

And then Kate was like are you okay and I was like I am sad all the time and she said I'm sorry and that was pretty much the end of that but I was really glad she was there.

> > >

To: davidsanders@Newcastle.k12.mass.edu
From: Sean_Cassidy@publaw.org
Subject: détente

Well, we appear to have reached some kind of truce around here, which of course is positive. Rosalind appears to be reconciled to her grounding. Of course, this is at least partly due to the fact that she believes she is fooling me by hanging out with her friends between the end of school and when I get home. I simply didn't have the energy to try and find supervision for her during this time, and I figured that having her think she's getting over on me would make her more tolerable when I was home. So far so good, though I do of course realize the inherent danger in these three unsupervised hours. But I do like to think I would know if she came home drunk, and if the high school experience is consistent with what it was twenty years ago, it's fairly easy for a 14-year-old girl to get booze at a party and much harder outside of the bacchanal setting. Please don't debunk this if you know it to be a myth.

On the anxiety front, I have found that it is no longer limited to times when I am actively worrying about Rosalind, but, rather, appears to be running in the background more or less constantly. So, for example, I will be sitting at my desk preparing some documentation for a civil rights suit, and my heart will hammer for twenty or thirty seconds, ending whenever I can force myself to take a deep breath.

I have actually seen a doctor, Grandmother, so you do not need to fret excessively over me. (I will add that while I appreciate the concern you expressed, it was really the idea of falling over dead and leaving Rosalind alone that was the biggest motivating factor in getting me into the doctor's office.) (Well, to be brutally honest, it was even more selfish than that. I don't want to die before my daughter loves, or at least likes, me. Somehow "beloved coworker, barely tolerated father" sounds like an unsatisfactory obituary.)

In any case, due to insurance or something, I have my third new doctor in five years, and, as it turns out, she is a very attractive woman whom I judge to be thirty years old. (Do not worry, Grandmother, for I have taken your advice and am through with doctors.) She informs me that I am experiencing stress-related heart palpitations. She wrote me a prescription for Ativan, warned me of its addictive potential, and sent me on my way.

I have yet to fill the prescription because I know myself well enough to know that I would begin worrying about developing a tranquilizer addiction in addition to everything else. I am also fairly certain that I would sing the Rolling Stones' "Mother's Little Helper" more or less constantly. Actually that started as soon as I got the prescription, to the point where Rosalind recently asked if torture was included in her grounding sentence. "Doctor pleeeeeeze . . ."

So, having failed with the medical route, I decided to try something more contemplative. I stopped off at Forest Hills after work the other day to visit Sandy and Eva's graves. I brought flowers and spoke to them for a few minutes. Well, that is sugarcoating it somewhat. Actually I brought flowers and tried to talk to them but mostly found myself crying—this is too hard, I can't do it, boo-hoo, et cetera.

Then they rose from their graves and attempted to eat my brain; no, actually, I felt nothing from their end. The dead in general are terrible conversationalists.

Nevertheless, I went back yesterday afternoon. I did not bring flowers because I am too cheap and/or lazy to do that on a regular basis. I walked around thinking and trying to get some insight into what they might do in my situation. Of course, if they were alive, this would not be the situation. This is the kind of thing that Rosalind is fond of calling a conundrum. In any case, I asked for assistance again and once again was appalled at what death has done to these women's social skills. But I did feel strangely calm as I walked around the cemetery. I don't know whether to attribute this to the intervention of friendly ghosts or to the tranquilizing power of good landscaping, but I will take it.

I am rambling and putting off some boring paperwork. Thank you, as always, for listening.

—Sean

> > >

To: Sean_Cassidy@publaw.org
From: davidsanders@Newcastle.k12.mass.edu
Subject: Re: détente

Grandmother? Grandmother! Well, I guess I'll take the ball-busting as a sign that you are doing better than you think you are, which is also what I think about your parenting, but far be it from me to spoil the pity party over there.

I'm glad you went to the doctor, but don't think I am buying this "I'm over doctors" bullshit, as you scope out Marcia version 5.0. (Yeah, I know 3.0 was a lawyer, Oedipus, and 2.0 was whatever the hell she was, a consultant or something, but you know what I mean. Go find a waitress to date and buy her a white lab coat if you have to indulge this thing. Jesus.)

My sister-in-law had a pretty serious trank jones, so I am not going to tell you to take the pills. I guess if the landscaping or friendly ghosts are doing it, then go hang out with the dead people. Just don't go all Harold and Maude on me.

Well, preparations are already under way for the big trek to Virginia for Thanksgiving. What are you going to do? Going to Philly?

—Dave

> > >

To: Rosalind9o@aol.com
From: Sean_Cassidy@publaw.org
Subject: True confessions

Rosalind—I have two things to tell you. Both of them spring from my recent trips to the cemetery to visit your mothers' graves. The first is that I thought I should offer to take you with me, or have you meet me there, or something. I have found, strangely, that being there actually lowers my stress level significantly. I thought you might, well, if not enjoy a trip there, then possibly like to have the opportunity.

Or possibly not. I visited my mother's grave three times and eventually stopped going because I didn't feel that she was there, and it depressed me.

Which brings me to my next point, or, rather, confession. It is likely that you will find this bizarre, corny, or stupid, but I did actually talk to your mothers while I was there. Now, I did not hear anything back from them, I got no messages from the other side that I need to relay, but it occurs to me that this shows that I am not the perfect cynic I described to you. That is to say, I don't really believe it's going to work, but I do it anyway. I don't know what this says about me, but there it is.

I should tell you, or, at any rate I want to tell you, and this is the kind of thing that I am never good at saying in person, that one of the things I did was to thank them for allowing me to be a part of this. I feel lucky to know you.

Ahem. In any case, let me know if you'd like to go with me. It's a very beautiful place.

—Sean

>>>

To: Sean_Cassidy@publaw.org
From: Rosalind90@aol.com
Subject: Re: True confessions

Sean,

Thanks. I mean, thanks for saying nice stuff about me. I mean, yes, I
do think you are a corndog ☺, but I used to hear a lot of nice stuff
about me all the time, and these days it's mostly about how I am
this problem child or whatever. So thanks.

    I don't really want to go to the cemetery, though. I don't know—
I don't feel like I need to be there to think about them, and I don't
want to go and just get sad. Thanks, though. I will let you know.

—R

ps—sometimes I talk to them too even though they never answer
me. I guess I am a chip off the old block or something.

        >>>

Dear Fluffy,
The grounding thing has actually been a boon to my social
life, and I like to say "boon" even though that is the name
of some tool administrator in the Charlesborough Public
Schools. But anyway, now I can sit with Sasha and Kristen
and Sara who I hate, I mean Sara is the only one I hate
sorry for the misplaced modifier or dangling or whatever

the hell, but anyway, I sit with them at lunch and then go
to the diner after school.

You will be happy to know that I stopped smoking. Jen
got suspended for three days apparently because she told
her guidance counselor to go fuck himself, and I decided
that the Alone Sad Girl pose kind of sucked in there, so I
just went and had regular lunch and kind of pretended to
be normal and yes it was just pretending, but I kind of
wonder if it's like crossing your eyes or something and you
get normal if you just pretend to be normal enough.

Anyway, since Charlesborough is smoke free I can't
smoke in the diner, and so if I have to go outside to smoke
that kind of defeats the purpose of being there and being
social, and that leaves home, but I don't really want Sean's
crappy lectures anymore.

The amazing thing I have to say is that today I don't
feel terrible. One thing is that Kate gave me this painting
she did of the girl in the glass cage, and it is really good,
and she was like I think you should have it and thank you
for taking me there because I got inspired and now I go
there all the time to sketch. All I could think is that she
and Sean are going to see each other there and that would
be pretty funny. Anyway, I really like Kate's painting. It
looks cool except that the glass is kind of breaking, and I
was like what is that, and she was like well, I felt bad for
her so I decided to bust her out of her cage. I am a dork so
I asked if she really did because that would mean she was
breaking shit at the cemetery, but she was like no, I just
did it in the painting and I felt like a total geek.

Which I guess if I can feel like a geek or like worry about feeling like a geek that is almost a normal thing, and like I said I feel like a pretty good imitation normal person today. I miss my moms but I don't feel like shit. I didn't do my homework, but I don't feel like crying, I just feel like somebody who had a day today instead of some sad girl who dragged her sorry ass through the day which is good, but I guess I worry a little bit about losing my sadness like Lisa said because that's sort of what I have that connects me to Mom and Mommy. Even though they would have been "in a state" if I had been all sad while they were alive, and they would want me to be happy, which I think is what Karen said to me when she was weeping one day, but anyway.

So the only bad thing is that I have like fries and a coke or now that it is getting a little nippy I will get a cup of coffee because that is a pretty good pose too but not as bad for you as smoking even though it gives you bad breath too.

But so I get home and I want something decent to eat, and all we have is this frozen vegan shit, which is okay and even good, but it doesn't feel like real food and even though I told Sean we always used to eat like this, I remember that we did at least used to have a real dinner on like Saturday or something, and we have basically never had one here.

So, anyway, I cooked dinner, which was not a big deal, it was some recipe in some hippie cookbook that Sean strangely has even though he obviously never cooks, since finding a pot was a big challenge, but anyway, I didn't

think it was a big deal, just some stuff from cans that I
mixed together in a pot, but Sean just about cried, actually
I think he did cry because he said he wanted to wash his
hands but then came back all red-eyed, so either he got
high in the bathroom which I doubt or else he was crying
for some reason. He was all like, "wow! this is really great!
I can't tell you how much I appreciate it!" and then he
kept saying that stuff over and over.

I kind of can't stand him when he is all goopy like
that. And maybe that is why the babes do not hang
around, because it's like he's this puppy dog that you kind
of want to kick, which is a mean thing for me to say about
him, and maybe I should stop but then again saying mean
shit about your parents is I guess what normal kids do so
there we go he is a goober.

> > >

Rosalind—

Under this note you will find a stack of vegetarian cook-
books. You should, of course, feel free to never look at them.
I certainly didn't bring you here to cook. Unless, you know,
you want to. So, if you want to, I thought I would facilitate
that for you by adding to our pathetic stock of one cookbook.
(This gem from the 1970's was left in my childhood home by
one of my dad's girlfriends. When I left home, I harbored
some illusions that I might someday learn to cook, so I took
our only cookbook. I am fairly certain that Dad never no-
ticed.) This cookbook is entertaining as an artifact of the

1970's—*please check out (and, hopefully, mock) the EN-
TIRE CHAPTER about how "smoking grass before a meal
brings you closer to the essence of the food," and subsequent
recipes for stoners with the munchies. Most of these seem to
involve at least a pound of cheese, which apparently was the
vegetarian standard in the 1970's.*

*So, in any case, if you find that you enjoy cooking, here
are some cookbooks (and, in the refrigerator, you will find
some actual vegetables that have not been processed into a
frozen or boxed entrée). I paged through some of them and
found some recipes that might be likely Thanksgiving win-
ners (I have decided to forgo the pathetic bachelor-size Butterball in honor of your vegetarianism). I thought we
might spend the day cooking some wild rice and cranberry
casseroles. Or something. Failing that, I also bought the full
Tofurky meal, which I must confess sounds vile, but I do
think it's important to have a backup plan.*

*Out of room on this paper and going on too much any-
way. Lawyer.*

—*Sean*

> > >

To: Sean_Cassidy@publaw.org
From: Rosalind90@aol.com
Subject: Thanks

Hey there, I got home from school a while ago and I wanted to say
thanks for the cookbooks. I did not notice the weed chapter before

you pointed it out, so now I am going to try it so I can get closer to the essence of my food. Don't have a heart attack, I am just joking.

Anyway, you were right that that was super cheesy and not just because every recipe has cheese in it, ha-ha. I am looking through all these and thinking about eating all this stuff, which is kind of a fun thing to do especially because no offense, but the stuff that comes wrapped in plastic was starting to get a little old.

Anyway, thank you, and don't worry I don't think you are trying to make me the scullery wench. Even though that is a pretty good phrase.

—R

> > >

To: Karenzallrite@msn.com
From: Sean_Cassidy@publaw.org
Subject: Rosalind—please read before deleting

Dear Karen:
Hello. I hope you are well.

I went to Forest Hills a few days ago to visit Sandy and Eva's graves, and, though this is not why I'm telling you this, I will say that I think you did a fantastic job picking the stones. They look great, and really put the others in that section to shame. Which, of course, is not why one buys a nice stone, but I am nervous and therefore babbling. Please bear with me.

So I went to Forest Hills not only to see the stones, but to ask Sandy and Eva for some assistance with Rosalind. I did not receive any direct response, but today it struck me that I was foolish to ask Sandy and Eva for assistance when you, being alive, are in a much better position to help. I hope that didn't sound flippant. I didn't intend it to.

This is obviously difficult for me. I understand that you were/are angry about my taking custody, and I know that our contact around Rosalind's nocturnal adventures was less than cordial. Still, we do both love Rosalind and want the best for her, even if we may disagree about what might constitute the best.

I know that you have been an important presence in Rosalind's life, and I am convinced that her dread at disappointing you has been a consistent positive force for her. Still, the fact remains that we have here a young woman who is having a very difficult time and making some bad decisions. I think it's to her benefit if we talk to each other about her rather than trying to glean whatever information we can by talking to her.

I guess I just feel that while I could certainly use some helpful insights, Rosalind would also benefit from having the adults in her life be on the same page.

Please let me know what you think, and thank you in advance.

—Sean

> > >

To: Sean_Cassidy@publaw.org
From: Karenzallrite@msn.com
Subject: Re: Rosalind—please read before deleting

Sean—
Okay. Much as it pains me to admit this, I do think you are right. I

worry about Rosalind all the time, and I would like to hear something from another adult, even yourself.

Sorry. That sounded petty because it was. So before we start
working together, as it were, I really feel that I need to clear the
decks emotionally. Otherwise, I will just be continuing to take pot-
shots at you as a way of venting the anger I haven't fully assimi-
lated.

So, let me say that I think your taking Rosalind was incredibly
selfish. I don't think it's best for her, and I don't think it's what
Sandy and Eva would have wanted. I think it's incredibly arrogant
for you to assume that the fact that you provided some ejaculate
fifteen years ago makes you in any way qualified to act as a parent
to a child you don't already know. Especially, I'm sorry, but here it
is, when there is someone who has known her her whole life who's
willing and ready to take her. If I didn't care for her so much, I'd
tell you to suffer on your own and go to hell.

As it is, you have selfishly, arrogantly, and unjustly taken this
child that I care very deeply for, and my feelings for her need to
take precedence over my feelings for you.

All right. Now that that is behind us, I can say that I am very
concerned about what Rosalind is telling me, or not telling me. She
seems to be drifting away from Sasha and her other friends, but
she hasn't said anything about who or what is taking their place.
Frankly, I'm afraid she's in the thrall of some kind of abusive
boyfriend or something—someone or something who can occupy
so much of her mental space that she can forget about her grief.
Did you know that forty percent of people who join cults are recently bereaved? I don't think that's an accident. There's a hole in
her life right now, and I would really like to know what's filling it,
but she won't tell me.

I guess that's about all I have for you right now, but I'd be interested to hear anything you have to say.

—Karen

   > > >

To: Karenzallrite@msn.com
From: Sean_Cassidy@publaw.org
Subject: Re: Re: Rosalind—please read before deleting

Karen—
I appreciate very much your willingness to set our differences
aside and proceed with the job of cooperating for Rosalind's benefit. I also do actually appreciate your willingness to put your feelings in the open rather than just taking digs at me for years. I
don't want to get into a long debate about what you've said about
me, but I guess I do have to say that I must cop to a certain degree of selfishness on my part. I am a single, childless (well, I used
to be, after a fashion) man in my mid-thirties, and, if I am honest, I
suppose I thought and still think that raising Rosalind, even for a
few years, will give my life some meaning and importance that it
doesn't otherwise seem to have. I know that you and I are of an
age and similar in our positions in life, and I suppose I would just
say I would be surprised if you didn't, on some level, have some of
the same motivations. Or perhaps I just assume that everyone else
shares my own failings. After saying that I wouldn't respond at
length, I find that I have, and so I suppose under the rules of en-
gagement here, you are entitled to respond to my response. And
then, hopefully, we can really put this behind us.

So—I have gone on at length about something I claimed I
didn't want to talk about because I have so little information
about what I do want to talk about. Here are some facts I have:

1. Rosalind has taken up smoking. Camel Reds—very fashionable.
2. Rosalind has been grounded since she and Sasha sneaked
    out of Sasha's house during a sleepover a week and a half ago.
3. Rosalind has begun cooking dinner every night, and when I
    get home from work, I frequently find the TV set to the Food
    Network. I have no idea what this information means.
4. I don't believe that many boys are calling here, though I
    have not taken the step of examining the incoming calls on her
    cell phone. This, by the way, reflects a lack of opportunity on my
    part rather than any kind of grand principle, as I no longer con-
    fiscate her phone the minute she walks in the door.
5. Having said that, I am not a hundred percent sure what she
    does with her after-school time. Except, as I suggested earlier,
    the evidence points to Emeril.

Thanks again, and I will continue to let you know what, if anything,
I find out. You do the same, and thank you.

—Sean

    > > >

To: Rosalind90@aol.com
From: Karenzallrite@msn.com
Subject: Thanksgiving

Hey Ros—I totally forgot when we spoke last night to talk to you
about Thanksgiving. As usual, I won't be returning to the family

compound in Cincinnati. I am going to attempt the famous Butterfield family jello salad, and I have laid in all kinds of provisions. If
you feel like spending the night, I've got some videos which we can
watch while eating my famous pumpkin pie. Anyway, I know that the
holidays are a tough time—already I feel a certain amount of sadness about the fact that we won't have your moms here for Thanksgiving, but I know that you and I can get through it together.

Love,
Karen

> > >

Dear Fluffy:
Well, I appear to have a bit of a conundrum here, or possibly I am impaled on the horns of the dilemma. This is
why I am still passing English. Actually I haven't told anybody but I might actually get a B because Westerberg
stopped me after class again which I hate and was like,
look I know you read everything because of what you say
in class, if you write me an essay I will give you a B minus
even though you haven't done any of the other ones, and I
don't know if he can do that but what the hell. I actually
kind of liked *To Kill a Mockingbird* even though I was
crying at the end like Sean or anyway some female dork
with the kids and their dad all "Thank you for my children Arthur." But anyway I am thinking about writing the
stupid essay like I said so I can not hear any more bullshit
about how I'm failing everything we're so worried about
you do you need a theraputic setting.

But anyway I was talking about my conundrum which is now I have two people expecting me for Thanksgiving and I don't really want to see either one of them but I have to pick one and then hurt the other one's feelings. At least Grandma isn't expecting me in Tampa and who knows whatever happened to Uncle Mike. If I stay here I will more than likely have Sean still going all googly about cooking, which he's been getting better about but whatever. Lisa says he is just happy that I am showing some interest in something that is not getting wasted or whatever but it's not like I am really that interested, I just like the way I can just kind of forget about myself for a few minutes while I am thinking about what to stir or chop or whatever, even though that risotto I tried to make was crunchy. But I don't know, Sean is all excited like I am going to be this master chef or whatever.

So if I stay here I will get/have to cook, which I don't know how I feel about that. But also I think it will be sad and weird because Thanksgiving was always such a big deal with like every gay person who doesn't talk to their family within a five-mile radius in the house, and either way it's not going to be like that.

But at least if I am at Karen's it will be kind of normal because she was always there so it will be like okay this is a little bit of what it used to be. But then again you can tell she's gonna get all weepy like she does practically every time I see her and we're gonna have to cry about how we miss Sandy and Eva so much, boo-hoo and so there won't be any way to pretend that this is my new life or whatever, it will just be like I have this fucked up old life even though the fucked up part is my new life and I don't even really know what I am saying.

I hate feeling like they both want something from me, like Sean is like, make my pathetic life complete and Karen is like, help me remember my best friends and I don't want to help anybody do anything because I am not doing such a shit hot job of helping myself these days, even though I guess I do have a real friend in Kate, I mean she has been e-mailing and calling which Jen never did and Jen is now like skipping school to hang out with the record store guy and whatever which means we see her only like twice a week and she always has forty-eleven CDs of like some new Polish punk band or whatever.

Kate burned me this metal CD which I didn't really like the first time I listened to it but I did appreciate it because except for when Sasha and Kristen came up all crying going we care about you I haven't had that much feeling like somebody cares about me and I know it takes five minutes to make a CD but at least you know some-body was spending five minutes thinking about you.

I don't know I don't know I don't have to make a deci-sion about that right now or maybe even ever so stop asking.

But I do have to decide where to go to Thanksgiving and I guess Karen will probably die or something if she has to spend it by herself and Sean is probably used to it so I guess I will go there but I actually do feel kind of bad for him but don't tell him because I have an image to protect, ha-ha.

> > >

To: Sean_Cassidy@publaw.org
From: Rosalind90@aol.com
Subject: Tofurky Day

Hey Sean. I am sorry to report that I think I am going to have
Thanksgiving with Karen. It's actually nothing personal and it's not
like I hate you or anything even though I think I did say that when
you grounded me, but you know I was just mad and also drunk. (and
by the way, am I ever getting un-grounded? I am just wondering)
It's just that I had Thanksgiving with Karen for as long as I remember, and I would just feel weird telling her no. Sorry again but if
you save the Tofurky maybe we can have it on Friday and it will be
like two Thanksgivings or something.

> > >

To: davidsanders@Newcastle.k12.mass.edu
From: Sean_Cassidy@publaw.org
Subject: I'm a loser, baby

. . . so why don't you kill me. Well, in answer to your question
about what our Thanksgiving plans are, I suppose we currently
have divergent plans. Which is to say that Rosalind is going to
spend Thanksgiving with her "aunt" Karen, who, as we know, is
not an actual aunt, not that I am entertaining any resentment
or bitterness.

      And yes, that is obviously a lie. I feel bitter and resentful, and,
as a nice bonus, I feel guilty for feeling that way because it reminds me that I did have selfish motives for initiating this whole
parenthood thing, which is to say that I thought I would no longer

have to spend Thanksgiving either alone or in the company of my father, which amounts to much the same thing and nearly always involves some sort of Hungry Man turkey dinner, which is so pathetic it makes me cringe.

So there you are. Rosalind is spending an important holiday with someone who has been important to her for her entire life, and this not only reminds me that I expected Rosalind to fill a hole in my life, but also that I have a long way to go before I get to the place where we have a relationship as real as the one she has with Karen. Or perhaps that will never happen. Perhaps she will leave for college—unlikely with her current grades, but let's assume she pulls it together at some point—and just never look back, and think occasionally of the strange four years she spent with that pathetic man trying to be her father.

I am sorry to be indulging in a pretty serious pity party—indeed, I think this might qualify as a pity bender—but I am trying my best to mask my disappointment in front of Rosalind, as I don't want to be imposing my needs on her when she has all she can do to keep herself afloat at this juncture.

I will end with some positive news, which is that I got a call from her English teacher, who praised at length her intelligence and insight and said that she wrote a fantastic essay on *To Kill a Mockingbird*. I was delighted to hear that it was fantastic, but I was ecstatic to hear that she had actually bothered to write an essay at all. So perhaps she is getting better.

Now if only I could do the same.

—Sean

> > >

To: Karenzallrite@msn.com
From: Sean_Cassidy@publaw.org
Subject: Thanksgiving

Hello there. Well Rosalind informs me that she will be joining you
for Thanksgiving. I had a brainstorm, which might be a bad idea,
but I did think I might run it by you. Perhaps the three of us could
spend the holiday together.

    I recognize that you and I are not exactly, or even inexactly,
friends, and indeed would probably never speak but for Rosalind,
but we do, as we've discussed, both care for her, and so I suppose
in some expansive definition that makes us like a family.

    (Indeed, if you and I could both get drunk and start yelling vul-
gar epithets at each other, it would be much like an actual family
Thanksgiving at Grandmother Cassidy's house that I remember all
too keenly.)

    In any case, I appreciate that Sandy and Eva's absence will be
especially glaring during this holiday season, and I certainly understand if you feel that the two of you need some time alone,
but please consider my offer.

Thanks,
Sean

> > >

To: Sean_Cassidy@publaw.org
From: Karenzallrite@msn.com
Subject: Re: Thanksgiving

Sean—

Even though I am pretty sure I never met your grandmother, I am
also sure I went to the exact same Thanksgiving dinner when I was
young. Was yours in Cincinnati? Did Uncle Jack throw a punch at
Uncle Rob?

In any case, I do appreciate what you are saying about how
we are stuck with each other. (You put it more nicely than that,
but I obviously don't have your talent for euphemism.) I do think,
however, that it's important for Rosalind and me to be together
and share our sadness this Thanksgiving. Thanks for your under-
standing.

—Karen

>>>

To: davidsanders@Newcastle.k12.mass.edu
From: Sean_Cassidy@publaw.org
Subject: Loser part 2

So immediately after sending you the pity bender e-mail, I sent
one to Karen, pathetically begging her to allow me to share their
Thanksgiving dinner, because apparently I do not have even a
shred of dignity.

And she turned me down, making me feel like even more of
a loser. I telephoned every homeless shelter in town and found

that they all have full staffs of volunteers for Thanksgiving, so I cannot even take that route to dodge the reality of my solitary Thanksgiving.

I suppose I could go to Philadelphia, but I am not quite emotionally prepared to face that alone. I am trying, instead, to look at this as an opportunity to rest up and regroup. That is to say, Rosalind will be Karen's responsibility for the night, so I will be able to exhale, relax, and watch football without fear of John Madden bringing up the sensitive subject of turduckens.

So there you have it. Did I mention that I will be dining on Tofurky? I suppose I could still snag the bachelor-size Butterball, but I feel like I've already spent the money on the complete Tofurky dinner, so I may as well enjoy, or at least consume it.

I hope you have a nice relaxing vacation and get lots of papers corrected . . . oh, wait, never mind.

—Sean

    > > >

To: Sean_Cassidy@publaw.org
From: davidsanders@Newcastle.k12.mass.edu
Subject: Re: Loser part 2

Ah, the old gym teacher joke. Feelin' like a loser, so make fun of the gym teacher. (You know I am actually making my students this year do a WRITTEN fitness evaluation, with lots of data from various activities they're doing over the course of the semester.) Ah, you sucked me in, you bastard.

Anyway, the bottom line is that Thanksgiving is just a day, and

you are going to have lots of days with her, and you'll be able to eat
all the gross vegetarian food you want, and I do think that this
time is going to be important to her, and she won't look at you like
some foster home she used to live in.

But you know that, anyway. So enjoy the football, and I am glad
to hear you're taking a break, because you need it. You also need a
date, my friend. It's been a while since you hit the magical six-
month barrier with, what the hell was her name? Oh, right, right,
Jan, trying to date the entire Brady Bunch, pathetic sitcom fixa-
tion, right right.

Anyway, maybe you should start trolling for Cindys.

Activate your online personal again.

Just an idea.

Well, we are off. Just in case you are feeling jealous of my wonderful family Thanksgiving, think about a nine-hour drive, then
think about Allie's horrible sister, no, not the hot one, stop asking
me about her, the hatchet-faced one who will give me her annual
lecture on the brutality of football and gender roles, blah blah blah
while you get to watch the Lions lose in peace. I think I would even
eat Tofurky for that pleasure.

—Dave

> > >

Dear Fluffy:
Well, Sean was pretty cool about the Thanksgiving thing,
but you could tell he was disappointed even though he was
trying really hard not to act disappointed, and I actually
did feel kind of bad which then I got mad about. I actually

called Lisa who is always giving me cards with her number like call me anytime, but anyway I actually did it this time and I said I was just feeling bad and she said that I need to take care of myself and that means not doing self-destructive stuff but also maybe not caring how somebody else feels for a while.

Done.

Which is lucky because I am just disappearing from lunch these days. I think Sasha kind of blamed me for her getting in trouble even though it wasn't my idea to go to that party or even my parent who caught us, though I guess it was my parent or donor guy whatever who actually stalked us to the party, so I guess I can give her that one, but anyway I feel like she has been kind of cold lately and that is actually okay because I don't know if we have anything in common except that we both liked this kid I used to be in the 8th grade. Who is probably gone forever. So mostly I just sit there and don't say much and I am thinking about if I can eat with Kate without the other bitches or maybe that Chris kid who I see and who was I guess along with Kate and Sasha and Kristen somebody who went out of his way to be nice to me, but he is always with his whole table full of guys and no way am I going to walk over there and have all them doing that goofy laughing thing all teasing him and whatever. Plus anyway the girls that hang out with them all tend to board too and wear that stupid skateboard uniform so maybe Abercrombie kids like me aren't welcome, even ones like me who are kind of like metal or at least mad and sad on the inside and not all pretty and windswept like those people in the

pictures in the store. Plus also I suppose a guy who is talking nice to a younger girl who is drinking at a party and
let's face it not all that good looking might not just be a
nice guy, or that's what Sean says which I guess is probably
true from what you hear.

Anyway, Kate said I was lucky to have two people
fighting over me for Thanksgiving because she hates
Thanksgiving or pretty much any time she has to spend
with her mom and stepdad and their kids they have together who according to her they obviously like better
than her.

I guess. Lucky is not really a word I would use to de-
scribe myself these days. But I guess I am lucky that I
found a friend and I am lucky to have a cool painting in
my room which Sean was like, hey where did that come
from, I like it, and I was like my friend did it, and he was
like, trying to be all casual, oh, which friend is that, and I
got mad and told him that my friends were my business,
which I guess is dumb because I could have just said Kate,
but you know that would mean like a million more questions where it would probably come out that I violated the
terms of my probation or whatever and then I really
would never get ungrounded. Aired? Atmosphered? There
ought to be a better word.

Well, happy Turkey Day Fluffy, or whatever, black
bean day or whatever we vegetarians say, I mean I will
take you along to Karen's mostly because I don't trust Sean
not to read you when I'm gone, but I don't think I will be
doing much writing. Mostly I will be eating and I hope

laughing but let's be honest here there are tears on tap for
this holiday and that is going to suck ass.

> > >

To: davidsanders@Newcastle.k12.mass.edu
From: Sean_Cassidy@publaw.org
Subject: Turduckens, Tofurky

Well, I bought myself a pie, and before I go for my second slice, I
thought I would take a break and tell you about my Thanksgiving.

I watched both the Lions and the Cowboys lose, and I don't
know what it says about me that I still enjoy it whenever Parcells
loses. Madden did, in fact, go on and on about the Turducken, as he
does every Thanksgiving, and so I was glad that Rosalind was not
here for that little halftime featurette, though she probably would
have been holed up in her room. Which, don't worry, I don't interpret as an alarming sign, as everyone tells me that every teenager
does that.

In any case, I was feeling somewhat guilty about the fact that I
hadn't even called Dad in, oh, I don't know, eight months or something, so I called him, and he did not actually appear to be intoxi-
cated, and I informed him that he has a granddaughter, and I was
surprised that he sounded so enthusiastic about the prospect.
That is to say, he sounded genuinely happy and said that he wanted
to meet her. I made vague, easily cancellable promises about how I
would check with Rosalind about her schedule and call him. (I am
sure she has a great deal of sulking scheduled, and I don't know if
that is a site-specific activity or if she could take it on the road.)

Hmm—that sounds particularly bitter toward both of my clos-
est relatives. Ah, well, I suppose a Thanksgiving alone will do that
to you. Although I will say that I was once again surprised by the
quality of the Tofurky meal. The stuffing was quite tasty. It's certainly not turkey, but it was salty and I ate far too much, so that is
about all I ask from a Thanksgiving meal.

Okay. To be fully honest, I am angry at Rosalind for leaving, I am
angry at myself for needing so much from a child, I am angry at
Karen because she is incredibly annoying and also transparently
needy, which I suppose I hate in her because it reminds me of me.
Did I mention the fact that I am angry at Dad for not giving me
the kind of upbringing that would make me want to call him more
than twice a year? And, of course, that I am angry with myself, because as I spoke to him and he was clear and coherent and nice and
slightly sad, I recognized that maybe I need to forgive him, which I
don't want to do.

Yes, I do need a date. Badly. I am firing up the online personal as
soon as I finish talking to you. And perhaps I will skip the second
piece of pie. Of course, the logistics of who would watch Rosalind
kind of elude me—would I ask Karen and thus go into favor debt
with someone I don't like? Would I leave her alone and thus guarantee some sort of teen bacchanal here in my own home? Well, I
suppose I really should procure the date first and work out the
logistics later. I plan to give prominent mention to my single fatherhood, hoping that will offset the lawyer-who-doesn't-actually-
make-a-lot-of-money factor, which has been such a stumbling
block in the past. (I know, Dr. Phil, it's about the kind of women I
date. You actually don't have to tell me that again, though I suppose if I do end up dating Marcia version 6.0, you will have earned
the right to tell me, oh, I don't know . . . 3 more times.)

I hope you got to enjoy Parcells losing (did you see him screaming at the wide receiver? I actually thought that vein in his head
might explode, thus ruining countless Thanksgiving appetites
throughout the country) without too much interference from your
hatchet-faced sister-in-law. Also, please tell me something about
the hot one besides that she is too young for me and lives in California. Humor me.

—Sean

> > >

Dear Fluffy,
It looks like I lied because I am here on Karen's couch
and it is one a.m. and I wanted to talk to you because this
Thanksgiving did actually suck ass but not exactly in the
way I thought it would.

It started out okay, we were doing a little bit of cooking and Karen was like, oh, I hear you're getting into
cooking these days, and I was kind of like well, where did
you hear that, and she got all embarrassed and said, oh,
well, Sean told me, and I was about to get mad about them
talking about me behind my back, but she beat me to it,
all, "I've been so worried about you, and even though I
don't really like him, so has Sean, and we were just ex-
changing a few e-mails about what was going on with
you," and I was pissed off and just didn't say anything.
I don't even know why I was so mad because it's not like
I've been lying to either of them unless being like I'll
be in my room and then sneaking out is a lie, which I

guess it is but I don't think it counts because I got
caught.

I guess I just thought being here would be a day off
from all that shit. And then later she tries with the thing
about do I have any special friends or whatever the stupid
boyfriend/girlfriend question is and since she is a lesbian
herself I can't use the heterosexist thing, and I don't even
know what to say. I wanted to tell her about Kate, I wanted
to tell her about Jen, about everything, about the diner, but
then I knew she'd run back and rat me out to Sean. I was
like, I don't know, I have some friends, I don't know if any
of them are special or whatever, and she was like well, you
don't have to decide that now anyway because you're supposed to be confused when you're fourteen, and I kind of
wondered if she'd been talking to Lisa too, but I guess
that's illegal or something.

Anyway it was wicked embarrassing and gross, and I
really thought there was a big teen sex talk coming which
I probably would have had to like die if that happened,
just crawl right into the oven next to the cranberry–wild
rice casserole and die of embarrassment, especially because you just know Karen would be all vagina power
which is gross but cool I guess but I just don't really think
I could have handled it just then or maybe ever from her.

So then dinner was fine, but you know Karen had like
two glasses of wine and even offered me one which I took
and felt okay, I mean it was different from sneaking Zima
in some kid's basement or something, it was like, oh, I am
a responsible grown-up now, which I thought was pretty
good because you know Sean would be all I can't trust you

with booze and never give me any wine with dinner even though I haven't ever seen him drink, but whatever.

But maybe Karen should take Sean's advice about the booze because she definitely had the weepy drunk thing going and she kind of lost her shit and I am there comforting her, like I'm this kid telling this grown-up it's going to be okay, there there, whatever, and then she starts crying about how unfair this is to me and she shouldn't be doing it, and I was like yeah, you got that right, but I didn't actually say that, I was just like well, whatever, and then she went to bed and here I am eating pie and writing to Fluffy and I swear to God I didn't even think about it until now that she is asleep with her weepy self, but I really miss them a lot tonight. I mean, even Karen losing her shit helped me not think about how this Thanksgiving is not like last Thanksgiving, and how, like, I don't actually have much to be thankful for and thankful to who, anyway, thanks God for killing my real parents and ruining my life, thanks a bundle, it's just like the Indians at Thanksgiving all thanks Great Spirit for bringing us these people who are going to kill us all. Fuck it.

The thing I hate is that I really felt like I was doing better, and now I feel like I'm doing worse, and I don't want to go to sleep and lie here with my brain going on and on about Mom and Mommy and I could watch one of Karen's videos but they are all stuff we all watched together which what the fuck was she thinking, well, I don't know. I want to go home, and I mean not Sean's house but my home my real home with the real family in it, except now there's some yuppie couple there with I swear to God some Porsche

SUV which Mommy would have slashed the tires if any-body ever drove up to our house in something like that.

Now I am actually kind of looking forward to school because at least there I can not think about all these fuck-ing grown-ups who are supposedly here to help me.

> > >

IM from Redchordfan03

Redchordfan03: R U THERE

Rosalind90: HEY KATE HOW WAS TURKEY DAY?

Redchordfan03: SUCKED BUT WHATS NEW

Redchordfan03: BUT SAW GRAMMA WHO LIKES ME BEST & HATES HANSEL&GRETEL STEPKIDS SO THAT WAS GOOD

Rosalind90: THAT'S COOL. SAW MY AUNT AND SHES STILL A MESS ABOUT MY MOMS

Redchordfan03: 2BAD ☹

Rosalind90: IT KINDA SUCKED BUT AT LEAST I COULDN'T GET SAD B/C SHE BEAT ME 2 IT.

Redchordfan03: I HATE HOLIDAYS

Rosalind90: ME 2 ☹

Redchordfan03: BUT THERES AN ALL AGES SHOW AT SOME VFW HALL OR SOMETHING IN FITCHBURG 2MORROW. 5 BANDS 10 BUCKS. WANNA GO?

Rosalind90: YEAH! BUT I GUESS I GOTTA FIND OUT IF I AM AIR-BORNE AGAIN

Redchordfan03: ?

Rosalind90: UNGROUNDED BY DONORBOY. I'LL GO ASK AND TELL U IN 5 MINUTES.

> > >

IM from Rosalind90

Rosalind90: HEY I KNOW THAT WAS ACTUALLY 2 HOURS R U STILL THERE?

Redchordfan03: YEAH—SO CAN U GO?

Rosalind90: YES! ☺ SEAN HAD TO CALL THE VENUE AND VISIT WEBSITES FOR EACH BAND AND DOWNLOAD COMMUTER RAIL SCHEDULES AND LIKE ASK EVERY BANDS MOM IF THEY WERE GOOD BOYS BUT YEAH I CAN GO

Redchordfan03: COOL. MEET U AT BACKBAY STATION AT 11 FOR 1105 TRAIN?

Rosalind90: BETTER MAKE IT QUARTER TO. THIS IS WICKED EMBARRASSING BUT SEAN WANTS 2 MEET U, PAT U DOWN FOR FLASKS, BRING DRUG SNIFFING DOGS, ETC.

Redchordfan03: WHATEVER I GUESS I'LL LEAVE MY CRACK PIPE AT HOME, HA-HA.

Rosalind90: SORRY HES SUCH A DORK HOPE U STILL WANT TO GO W/ME.

Redchordfan03: OF COURSE. ITS DORKY BUT KINDA CUTE. I COULD TELL MY MOM I WAS GOING DOWNTOWN TO TURN TRICKS CUZ IM JONESING AND SHED BE LIKE WHATEVER IM BUSY WITH THE TWINS.

Rosalind90: SORRY.

Redchordfan03: THANKS. WHATEVER, SUFFERING MAKES BETTER ART OR SOMETHING.

Rosalind90: C U 2MORROW AT 1045!

Redchordfan03: ILL BE THE ONE IN THE RED CHORD SHIRT HA HA.

>>>

To: Karenzallrite@msn.com
From: Sean_Cassidy@publaw.org
Subject: advice

I hope you had a nice Thanksgiving. I quizzed Rosalind about it but she was not forthcoming. Did you get any good information out of her? More specifically, did you get anything about somebody named Kate?

I ask because Rosalind asked me if she could go to some kind of all-ages metal show in Fitchburg (!) at some VFW hall with Kate, and, after calling the VFW hall and speaking to several very sullen veterans, I did ascertain that it's actually happening, and that it's an all-music, no-booze kind of affair. I also checked some of the bands' websites and found really appalling lyrics about dead bunnies and eating the dead and such like things, but for some reason this didn't really alarm me. I downloaded a map of Fitchburg and figured out where the hall is and called my colleague who grew up there and asked if two teenage girls would be safe walking there, and she said yes.

I also said that I needed to meet Kate before I gave my approval for her to get on the train with her for this little adventure, and she practically died of embarrassment but agreed to the condition.

So I feel like I have pretty much all of my bases covered, except I know from my own experience that many bad apple teens are particularly adept at charming the socks off of adults. (The kid who supplied coke to about a third of the student body at my school was much beloved by faculty and parents alike, so much so that our principal tried to get him to say it had all been a tragic mistake when his supply fell from his bookbag.) So I wanted to know if you had gleaned any information about Kate.

   Also, though I can't undo my decision at this point without starting a civil war in this house, this is the right thing to do, right? I have to allow her to have a life. Right? Anyway, any information you can provide would be most appreciated.

—Sean

   > > >

To: Sean_Cassidy@publaw.org
From: Karenzallrite@msn.com
Subject: Re: advice

Sean—Thank you for keeping me in the loop and for asking about our Thanksgiving. It was uneventful—we ate too much and got sad. I'm sorry to say that I couldn't really get anything out of Rosalind about Kate or much of anything else. She told me she has "some friends," but "nobody special," which probably means she has a crush on at least three people instead of one. So I can't tell you anything about Kate. Hopefully you can tell me once you meet her. I will say that Rosalind seemed slightly better than she had in the past, and she really did enjoy the cooking. I am happy to see her involved in something that involves creation and, ultimately, nurturing, though of course I worry about her falling into some societally programmed femme-y gender role thing.

   As for your decision to allow her to go fifty miles on the train with someone you don't know to some horrible concert, I have

pretty mixed feelings. On the one hand, I can see that using per-
mission to do this thing as leverage is going to get you a face-to-
face with somebody who seems important to Ros, which I do think
is important because we are in the dark about who she's hanging
out with and we need not to be.

On the other hand, I hate to see her go to something like this
with such horrible music. It's just a cauldron of negative energy,
and I really think Ros needs positive, life-affirming experiences
right now instead of a celebration of negativity. Also, I don't know
if you read about the fires at Lollapalooza several years ago, or the
fires and rapes (!) at Woodstock. This kind of music feeds into a,
and I'm sorry here, but particularly male strain of aggression that,
like all male aggression, always finds its way to violence against
women. I am frankly worried about putting Rosalind into that kind
of environment. I hope it's not a mistake.

—Karen

> > >

To: davidsanders@Newcastle.k12.mass.edu
From: Sean_Cassidy@publaw.org
Subject: Fwd: Re: advice

Dave—Attached find the latest e-mail from Karen. I thought
maybe we could introduce her to your hatchet-faced sister-in-law.
It appears they might hit it off.

Anyway, I am sorry to clog up your in-box with a hundred messages for you to get when you get back from Virginia, but I did
need to tell you about meeting Ros's friend.

Well, just to jump ahead, Rosalind went fifty miles on the commuter rail to some all-ages metal show in Fitchburg and returned safely, arriving at the Back Bay station at 8:30 pm on Saturday. Her concert review: "It was cool."

As a condition of her going to the headbanger's ball, I said I wanted to meet her friend Kate who was accompanying her. So we met at the station and I bought everyone coffee, and we sat for a few minutes while I interrogated Kate and Rosalind attempted to melt under the table with shame.

I am, of course, wary of the adult-bullshitting powers of many teens, but I have to say that this kid seemed okay. She was dressed really appallingly—well, all in black, with fishnet stockings and combat boots, which I guess is a look, but she seemed like a sweet, gentle kid. She said she'd been going to Forest Hills to sketch a lot, and she showed me some of her sketches, which were really good. I told her I'd been there recently too, and she said yeah, Rosalind had taken her there a couple weeks ago, at which point I believe Rosalind attempted to kick her, because of course she had just blown Ros's cover about after-school time while she was grounded.

I feigned obliviousness, though, and moved on to the next question, which was about which bands she liked. She listed a whole raft of bands, of which Metallica was the only one I had heard of. I said I liked *Master of Puppets* but thought their lyrics were often kind of clumsy.

I do believe Rosalind actually briefly died at that point, but she quickly revived and started looking very theatrically at her watch, which prompted me to say something about how they didn't want to miss their train, and have a good time, et cetera.

I have to say, I felt like superdad on several counts. For one thing (after she arrived home safely and not obviously chemically

altered in any way), I allowed her to do something that actually
sounded like fun (I mean, obviously, it sounded like it would have
been fun when I was fourteen. I think I'd prefer all kinds of dental
surgery to spending an afternoon listening to bad metal in a VFW
hall with angry teens all around me), and I actually met one of her
new friends. I know this is a good thing because a handsome star
of an NBC television show told me I should meet my child's friends.
The More I Know . . . Ahem. Finally, I was happy, though this has
nothing to do with me, that Ros appears, without any input from
me or Karen or pretty much anyone, to have made a good choice
of someone to hang around with.

Perhaps things are looking up.

I recognize as I write that that you are going to receive all of
these e-mails at once and probably think I am even more insane.
"Everything's horrible! No, everything is great!" Well, I suppose I'm
just happy to be able to say that something good is happening.

—Sean

> > >

To: Sean_Cassidy@publaw.org
From: davidsanders@Newcastle.k12.mass.edu
Subject: Re: Fwd: Re: advice

Well, that was a hell of an e-mail bonanza this morning! And thank
you for the e-mail attachment. I love the part about "particularly
male aggression." Allie's hatchet-faced sister would really like that,
but I do have to say she seems to have given up on the whole football thing. I volunteered to wash dishes before watching the game,

and that seemed to calm her down a little. And yeah, I thought the Tuna's head was going to explode on that blown TD reception, and yeah, it's probably unhealthy for us to still hate Parcells, but that's what football is for.

Speaking of Thanksgiving, my friend, you have something to be thankful for, which is that Allie's hot sister (Sorry—not named Cindy, though she is Kimberley, which was the girl from *Diff'rent Strokes*, I think) is applying to law schools in Boston. Allie obviously lost her mind and did nothing but talk about how great you were, how you'd been to BC law, blah blah blah, and how she should come up so we can all get together, blah blah blah. Did I mention that Kimberley has been working as a yoga instructor? I probably shouldn't even tell you this stuff, but I am feeling nice and thought you might enjoy imagining what that kind of flexibility could mean to you.

So I will let you know when she hits town. She is 26 and so way too young for you and will probably go for some buff rock-climber or something, but at least you've got some hope. For me it would be kind of ideal because I know she's nothing like Marcia (okay, okay, she got all gooey about your little save-the-world job, which is something else I probably shouldn't tell you because you'll start stalking her), but she's still a lawyer, or at least a lawyer-in-training so I can still tease you about the Oedipus thing.

So overall, Thanksgiving was pretty painless, except for the traffic on the way back which was horrible, and Max was an incredible pain in the ass the whole way. I really thought I was going to kill him somewhere around hour 5.

Sounds like you had an eventful weekend. For the record, I think you did the right thing letting her go and probably by interrogating her friend too, even though you did expose her to particularly male aggression. (If you ever get the chance, you could tell Karen that I break up probably four fights a year, and the girl vs. girl ones are always the bloodiest, most vicious, and hardest to break up. Usually the boys are happy if they have shown that they are willing to throw a punch, whereas the girls "ain't stopping until the fucking bitch is dead!" That's actually a quote.)

Anyway, it sounds like things are looking up, or at least not down. Keep it up. Speaking of which, just because I love you, I attached a digital picture of Kimberley from this weekend. What you do with it is your business. You filthy pervert.

—Dave

> > >

Dear Fluffy,

The concert was great! Well, I mean, the whole day was great except for Sean's horrible job interview thing with Kate, which yes the worst part was when we got on the train and she was like, "I don't know why you say he's such a dork. He seems cool to me," and all I could say is like well, you don't have to look at the screws in your window frame every day, and she was all TAKING HIS SIDE, like, "he was probably just worried," and I swear I started to wonder if she had a crush on him or something but that was way way too gross a thought, like probably grosser even than any other thought I ever had, so I changed the subject.

We had a great train ride just laughing and talking and making fun of people which there were a lot of people to make fun of on the train. These two old guys kept going, "Eyyyyyyy . . . BOB!" Nobody knew who Bob was, and me and Kate almost died laughing.

Anyway, the concert was in some gross place and it was so loud that I still can't really hear right, but I actually got into it way more than when I just listened to the CD. It was like I could just forget everything and all that volume and anger or whatever (or "negative energy," which is what Karen couldn't shut up about on the phone tonight) just made me feel really good. Which is weird because you would think that it would make you feel worse and more sad and angry but actually I felt better and happier than I have in a long time at the end.

We hung out for a little while with this one band called Child Soldiers Run Amok where Kate's cousin Jamie is the bass player, and the lead singer was talking about how he was straight edge, which I had no idea what he was talking about but I guess it means he doesn't smoke or drink or anything. Kate said he used to smoke like a chimney but he got TB like it's 1826 or something and they told him he'd die if he smoked, so he got straight edge or something. Which it was a little disappointing to find out it was not really some strong belief or something because I thought it would be cool to have that kind of thing and just not care what everybody else thought. Plus, yes, he was really cute but too old for me even though he is six years younger than Jen's boyfriend.

I think Karen would probably kidnap me and have me deprogrammed if I went out with some 19-year-old metal singer, not to mention Sean would embarrass me to death, all, "Oh, I like Metallica, but the lyrics are clumsy and I don't think the Lovecraft stuff works." Jesus. What a dork.

Anyway it's not like we have to worry about this particular scenario because it's not like the guy noticed I existed at all with Kate there which who can blame him but whatever.

On the way home something funny happened where Kate said that she still really liked and cared about Jen, like I guess they've been friends since grade school, but now she was just worried about her and didn't really like who she hung out with, and I was like I bet Sasha is saying the exact same thing about me right now somewhere and that is some kind of irony but at least not cruel.

And that is all the interesting news from my day except Sean was like I really think your friend seems like a neat person when he picked me up, and I totally wanted to be like yeah well she boosted some tampons from the CVS on the way to the train station, but then I do actually want to get to hang out with her again, so I shut up.

ps.——five minutes later

Oh my God, I just had that day. I mean I am just sitting here typing to you Fluffy and I realize that I just had that day that Lisa said I would have where I didn't miss my

moms all day long. I mean, I guess it's because I was busy
or whatever, but wow. Wow. I am kind of trying to make
myself feel sad or guilty about it, but I kind of can't and
I don't care. There's always tomorrow.

> > >

To: Karenzallrite@msn.com
From: Sean_Cassidy@publaw.org
Subject: Kate

Well, Rosalind survived the trip to Fitchburg unscathed, and I did
actually meet the mysterious Kate. Overall, I got a good impression. I mean, yes, she is into metal and dresses in all black, but she
seems like a good kid. She is a very talented artist, which I recognize is not a guarantee of being any kind of decent person, but it
does at least seem that she has an outlet that she spends a great
deal of time on, which would seem to preclude heavy drug use,
shoplifting, murder, etc.

Overall, I feel very good about them hanging out together.
Actually I liked her better than Sasha, who I admittedly saw at
a point in time when she was not her best but who seemed kind
of aggressively bland to me.

So that is the report. Did you hear anything?

> > >

To: Sean_Cassidy@publaw.org
From: Karenzallrite@msn.com
Subject: Re: Kate

Sean—

Thank you for the update. I got very little about the concert. I expressed my concern about her immersion in the culture of negativity around that kind of music, and also the aggression and violence that goes with it. She didn't say much, but made some kind of unsophisticated argument about catharsis.

I hit such a brick wall the last time I asked a direct question about Kate that I decided to tiptoe around the subject, which got me exactly the same amount of information as the direct question. So much for subtlety. All I can say is that if this girl Kate is immersed in this negative, violent subculture, she is more than likely a victim of abuse. I feel for her, but I worry about her influence on Rosalind if she is acting out her reaction to abuse with this kind of self-annihilating, violent, anti-woman subculture.

I can see that she charmed you because she is "edgy," but let's be mindful that that edge can cut both ways.

—Karen

> > >

To: davidsanders@Newcastle.k12.mass.edu
From: Sean_Cassidy@publaw.org
Subject: Kimberley

Okay, the joke's over. No, I mean, really. I got an e-mail from Kimberley asking for advice on housing and The Law, and all I can say
is that if this is an elaborate prank, please call it off immediately,
because I am running around like I am fifteen years old, my head
filled with daydreams of varying erotic intensity. I mean, nobody is
"really interested in public-interest law," especially nobody who
looks like that.

　　Right?

　　In all seriousness, I don't exactly know what to do—I don't
want to respond immediately and appear too eager and desperate
(or, more accurately, as eager and desperate as I actually am), nor
do I wish to appear too aloof.

　　Ugh. I am a mess. Thank you!

—Sean

　　> > >

To: Sean_Cassidy@publaw.org
From: davidsanders@Newcastle.k12.mass.edu
Subject: Re: Fwd: Dave's sister-in-law

Oh, I wish I could tell you it is a joke, but it is all too real. I know nobody is interested in public-interest law. What can I tell you, insan-
ity runs in that family: hatchet-face we can just take as a given,
Tim goes rock-climbing with juveniles convicted of violent crimes,

Allie fell for me, and Kimberley wants to be a public-interest lawyer and really wants to meet a guy nine years older than her with no money and a fourteen-year-old daughter. She'll be here in January. Send her an e-mail. Tomorrow. I agree that revealing your true desperation could be a deal-breaker at this point.

You're welcome.

—Dave

> > >

To: Redchordfan03@aol.com
From: Rosalind90@aol.com
Subject: My dorky poem

Okay, so I got kind of inspired or whatever after the concert. I decided to write a poem, which I know is probably horrible, but since you gave me a painting with this on it, I thought I would send you my pathetic attempt at poetry. Which I am also going to give to Westerberg for extra credit or something because I figure if I can cultivate a tortured artist image with him it can only help my grades. (And yeah, doing some math homework would help my grades too, but that doesn't seem to be happening.)

Anyway, here's my poem:

Girl in a Cage

Girl in a cage
Guards her own grave
She's safe from the wind and the rain

They carved her from rock
And set her on top
She's a monument to their pain

While six feet below
Where the coffin-worms go
There's a cage of a different kind

With some shards of bone
And a scrap of her dress
Which is all that she's left behind

Two girls in two cages
But there's no girl at all:
To say that she's here is a lie

No cage can protect you
The future neglects you
And everything ends when you die.

Okay, so maybe that is a little bit morbid or depressing or whatever, which is kind of funny because I am not feeling too morbid or
depressed right now, but anyway, there it is.

Tell me what you think, unless you hate it.

—R

> > >

To: Rosalind90@aol.com
From: Redchordfan03@aol.com
Subject: Re: My dorky poem

Ros—I really liked it! I think it is really good! I don't think it's dorky, and I don't think it's too morbid, but then I draw skulls and go to the cemetery all the time, ha ha. Thank you! Can I send it to my cousin Jamie? I think he might like it.

　　Hey Jen invited me to go to hang out with her and her boyfriend at her house tomorrow after school. Do you want to go? I kinda don't but I would feel bad blowing her off, but her boyfriend is kind of creepy and I would like some company. So what do you say?

—Kate

　　> > >

New text message!
From: Rosalind cell
4:30 pm
911 PLS CALL MY CELL N ACT MAD, WHRE THE HLL AM I, ETC.. IN A BAD SITCH. I NEED AN EXIT. THTS A MATRIX JOKE.

　　> > >

Dear Fluffy,
Greetings from the New Jersey Turnpike! Sean is in line at Sbarro and I am sitting here with dorks staring at me like

they never saw a girl typing before, which maybe they haven't.

Anyway, Sean is kind of my hero even though we are now doing something weird and I kinda wonder if he's losing it. So me and Kate and a bunch of other people went to Jen's boyfriend's house and it was cool I guess but Kate is right the guy is creepy which I guess news flash that some twenty-five-year-old dating a junior in high school is creepy, but he just made me really uncomfortable but I didn't feel like I could leave and then they got high and I kind of passed it past me if you know what I mean because I was wicked uncomfortable and I wanted to be in control because like I said this guy Carsten was creepy and he had other creepy pedophile buddies there and even some older girls who were like gonna claw our eyes out because we were on their turf like we wanted those gross guys or something. Anyway after the weed which I noticed Kate also passed up, Carsten was like well now let's make it interesting and he starts fishing out some little plastic bags which I don't know what was in them but it wasn't something I wanted to be involved in and Jen was like frenching him and horrible Polish punk music was play- ing and I was like I have to get the fuck out of here but I don't know how to do it so I sent Sean a text message like call me and act mad and he did a great job.

Well, he did a terrible job acting mad because he was all like "Are you safe, what's going on?" and I had to be like, "God! I told you I'm just in the basement, I can't hear the house phone, stop calling me every five minutes!" and he was all like "should I call the police?" and I'm all "NO! I am in the house, I swear!" And he was like, "Okay, I'm coming to get you, where are you, and I was like all sarcastic, "Yeah, okay, I'm going to run down to Ashmont and get the T so I can get home before you're off work, because I'm out partying in the middle of the afternoon!" and he was like, "I will be at Ashmont in ten minutes," and I felt so relieved but I had to be like, "Fine!"

So then I was like hey everybody I'm technically grounded and I have to actually bust my ass home and Kate jumped up like she shouldn't walk to Ashmont alone so I will take her and we like ran out of there and then Sean pulled up at Ashmont and Kate was like oh my God you set that up and that is so cool your dad is so cool to come and get you, blah blah blah and I swear she ought to move in with him and I will go be less loved than the twins and her folks probably wouldn't even notice.

Damn that pizza line is long. I am starving. And there are like a million screaming little kids in here.

Anyway, we dropped Kate off and then Sean was all I'm so proud of you for calling me and I liked your Matrix joke and I'm glad you feel that you can count on me and all this stuff which I was just like shut up.

And then it was all why are you in this situation on a Friday afternoon, did Kate invite you there, were people getting high, you smell like weed, were you getting high, and I was like, look, I called you because I wanted to get out of that situation which maybe shows that you should trust me!

He was like, yeah, okay, but let's go home and pack

because we are going to Philadelphia for the weekend. I guess we are going to see my famous stoner grandpa so I will be scared straight or something which is so dumb because I already just said no and even if I didn't it's not like meeting some old guy is going to make me change my evil ways. Sean says no, he was planning this anyway and I was like yeah, that's why you never told me but whatever.

Here he comes with pizza, finally.

> > >

To: davidsanders@Newcastle.k12.mass.edu
From: Sean_Cassidy68@yahoo.com
Subject: On the Road Again

Greetings from the New Jersey Turnpike! I am at this internet kiosk in a service area between the Sbarro and the convenience store. Why am I here, you ask? I'm taking Ros to visit Dad, which he and I had spoken about, but also because Ros gave me this emergency call to get her from some drug den this afternoon, and I just felt like she needed to see what several decades of drug use can do. Or else maybe I'm impressed by her courage and I'm taking her to do this thing I don't want to do because I want backup. Okay, I have no idea why I'm doing this. It just seemed like the right thing to do.

Even though I was incredibly proud of her for messaging me to come and get her and I did actually believe her when she said she was not high. She also made this joke in the message—well, anyway, I loved that she made the joke, I loved that she called me when she was in trouble. Basically I love this kid so much it's scary.

And she is glaring at me now, so I suppose we should go. I will let you know how it goes with the old man.

>>>

Dear Fluffy:

It is Saturday morning and I am alone in this gross apartment which I kind of can't believe Sean grew up here because he is so neat and everything. Sean and Niall are out getting breakfast or so the note says and I am calling him Niall because I met him last night, well, anyway, let's see.

We got in here at like midnight and Sean found the key where it was hidden and he was like it's amazing nobody has broken in here, that's my key that I hid here in 1984. He said his dad couldn't get off too early because of the short notice but told us to come in and make ourselves at home.

So we like clear a space on the couch and start watching TV, and I swear to God Sean was asleep in like five minutes. At like one o'clock Niall who I guess is my grandfather came home and he was pretty much like Sean described him with this gray beard and everything.

He was like, so I guess you're Rosalind, and I was like so I guess you're my famous stoner grandfather, and he laughed and laughed but Sean didn't wake up, and so he was like, I'm starving, you wanna go get some cheese fries, and I'm like, okay, fine.

So we go to this place which is like full of drunken frat boys and me and Niall which is what he told me to

call him, and we get these cheese fries, which were really
good so we actually got two orders, and he was like, "So,
do you hate him?"

And I was like, "Sean?"

And he's like, "Yeah, because he hates me for being
the one who lived," and I was like actually I think he hates
you because you were high all the time or anyway that's
what he says.

And he got kind of sad looking and he was like, yeah,
I did a shitty job, but Sean is an old soul, he didn't really
need any parenting, the kid parented himself right into
law school, where I'm a really young soul and so I needed
to kind of follow my bliss for a few years.

I didn't really have anything to say about that. But I
said I don't hate Sean but he does get on my nerves and
I miss my moms a lot.

He was like, yeah, well, this will define your life for a
while but don't let it get in the way of following your
bliss, because your bliss is still there.

I didn't know what the hell he was talking about, but I
kind of nodded because I liked hearing him talk. He said
how he doesn't actually smoke anymore and asked me did
I smoke and I was like well, I haven't but I am keeping my
options open, and he was like that's so good, don't close
yourself off to experience, but then he was like he felt like
this fog in his brain lifted when he stopped smoking and
how he was writing this novel that he thinks is what he
was always meant to do or something.

Then he told me some stories about Sean as a little kid

that were pretty funny. Then I was tired and really thirsty
from all those fries, and I was like I need to hit the sack,
and so we went back.

I don't know—I like him. I mean, I don't know what
Sean thought was the point here, because I was not like oh
my God this is so horrible I never want to turn out like
this guy or anything. It's not like he smells and lives in a
shelter or something. He's just this old guy who I guess is
a little more cool than most people's grandfathers. I mean
it's not like he falls asleep and golfs which is what I think
grandfathers do, but I guess I only know that from TV,
since Mommy was excommunicated or whatever by her
parents and obviously I never met Grandpa Joe but he did
die on a golf course so there you go.

> > >

TRUTH IS BEAUTY BAR AND GRILL
A NOVEL
BY NIALL CASSIDY

> > >

Chapter 24

It was four o'clock on a Wednesday afternoon. I was drying
glasses. I was just about to wrap my brain around the depths
of *Tarkus* that had always been obscured when a girl who
couldn't have been seventeen came in and sat down at the

bar. She looked vaguely familiar, but I couldn't imagine how I knew her. I saw a kid this age about once a year in here, and I always abused the hell out of them, like I was about to do to her.

"You know, this is just depressing," I told her. "What are you, about sixteen? And you're about to whip out some piece of shit fake Missouri license or something, right? Can we just skip this part? Isn't there some latchkey kid's basement you could be drinking in?"

"Well, I guess he got the asshole part right," she said. "Listen, Jack, I'm not here to drink. You are Jack, aren't you?"

"I don't think I know you. Should I?"

"Probably. I'm your granddaughter."

Well, that would explain why she looked familiar—those were her grandmother's eyes boring into me. She might not have been here to drink, but now I damn sure needed one. I poured myself a Maker's Mark and took a gulp. "I guess Alan's been busy since I saw him last," he said.

"Kind of. It's a complicated story. Anyway, he says you're an asshole and a drunk. I guess I wanted to find out for myself."

"Well, I guess I'm guilty on both counts. How is Alan doing, anyway?"

"He's okay, except I guess I'm giving him fits or something. I'm some kind of problem child. I guess I'm kind of fucked up since my moms died."

"Hey, I'm sorry, kid. How old was your mom?" I was sorry for the kid. I hated to see my dead wife's eyes looking sad. I was also sorry for myself for everything I didn't know about my son. He lost a wife and didn't even invite me to the funeral? Not that I would have wanted to go, but I would have liked the invite.

"One was forty-two, the other was forty-six." I didn't know what the hell she was talking about. My world in here was pretty small, but I suppose that outside, things were different. I couldn't imagine what the arrangement was here, and it seemed like a waste of time to try and figure it out.

"I'm sorry. I guess losing one mom is hard enough."

"I don't have to tell you, do I? Look what it did to Alan. And you. Or anyway, Alan says your wife bit the dust, you upped your drinking a notch, started chasing pussy like they were about to make it illegal, and generally fucked up your life."

Well, that hurt. I suppose if I had really thought about it, I would have figured that was what he thought of me, but it was still kind of shocking to hear it right out there like that. "I guess that's more or less right. The pu ... uh, the ladies actually pursued me, but I guess I found out what they were really chasing when I stopped dealing weed. All of a sudden I was a lot less interesting. Then I woke up one day and found I had gray hair and this." I patted my substantial gut. "But I don't have any regrets about the life I chose. Now Alan, on the other hand, puts on a tie every day, puts on that uniform of conformity and American 'success,' marches in to serve his corporate master, and lets other people run his life. He lives for money and the approval of a corrupt society. I live for myself. You tell me who's fucked up."

She looked at me with those sad, familiar eyes and

stood up. "If you ask me, old man," she said, "you both are."

Without saying good-bye, she walked out of Truth Is Beauty and into the hot Philadelphia afternoon.

> > >

To: davidsanders@Newcastle.k12.mass.edu
From: Sean_Cassidy68@yahoo.com
Subject: My big weekend

Well, it is Sunday night and we are back from Philadelphia. It was a hell of a trip. I hardly know where to begin. All right. I will begin with the most important part. I seem to have reconciled with old Niall. On Saturday morning Rosalind was sleeping in, and we went out and ate scrapple and just talked things out. Or, rather, I talked and he listened. I said that I felt bad for not talking to him, that having Rosalind around has made me reevaluate things, and one of the things I've decided is that I don't want to be a stranger. I didn't say this, but I have been feeling increasingly embarrassed about my estrangement from Dad since Rosalind arrived. How do I explain that I have a living parent that I choose not to speak to to someone who lost two? It seems wasteful.

I then laid out this catalog of his parenting failures, and he nodded calmly and did not dispute any of what I had to say. He asserted that he has a young soul, whereas I have an old one, and that if I look at my life I seem to have done okay, while he is still in pretty much the same place he's been for thirty years, with the exception of some semi-autobiographical novel he claims to be writing.

I think what he was essentially offering was the "Boy Named

Sue" defense: I resented him, but his neglect helped make me strong and successful and to realize that I could not depend on other people. I suppose I can see that point of view, but I think it's a cop-out and a fraud on his part.

But, surprisingly, I didn't say that. I just said that I wanted to stop dwelling on the past and have a future with my daughter in which he was a part of our lives. But that he was not allowed to ever talk to me about *Tarkus* again. He appears to be able to live with that.

Now, of course, the question is whether I can. As much as Rosalind's presence reminds me that I need to have some contact with him, every time I make an attempt to be a parent to her, I feel the anger that he didn't make the effort for me.

Rosalind says she believes he actually did the best he could, but that, to judge by the condition of the apartment and the information she gleaned about his last twenty-six years, his best simply wasn't very good. Perhaps that's true too. Apparently they had some sort of late-night heart-to-heart, and she came away from it really liking him. He told her to follow her bliss, and she seems to be contemplating what exactly her bliss is. I suppose this is an okay activity for a teenager, as long as she arrives at different conclusions about the nature of her bliss than old Niall did.

We spent a fair amount of time walking around the old neighborhood, just the three of us, looking at all the old sights. It is difficult to find a lot of the stuff I remember because Penn has done so much construction in the last few years. Fortunately, the law school is much the same, so we walked over there, and I remembered sitting on the steps with Dad waiting for Mom to come out of class. That was a nice time. Or so it seems. Perhaps everyone thinks that way about when they were seven. I must confess that I did get somewhat annoyed with old Niall. It seems that every block in Philadelphia contains a Niall Cassidy History Spot, and so he was regaling Rosalind with tales of the party at this house, the crazy woman he dated who lived down there, the time he was shot at over there, et cetera. Objectively speaking, it was entertaining, but I couldn't help thinking that he was out getting material for his wonderful geriatric tales while I was home by myself trying to be my own parent.

But, as I said, I am trying to put that behind me. It is just much easier said than done.

In any case, we agreed to get together for Christmas, and he promised to write regularly. I offered to get him a computer, but he said that he was too old a dog for such a new trick. (I resisted telling him that personal computers have been around for more than twenty years and therefore hardly constitute a new trick.)

Rosalind and I had a nice conversation on the way home today. I think she was relieved to have something to discuss besides her troubles, and she happily gave me her perspective on Niall. She asked to play this cassette he had given her of *Tarkus,* and I told her that it might cause me to drive off the road and that, further, she was never to play it in our home without headphones or mention the subject to me again. I could almost see her filing *Tarkus* away in the "ammunition" file. I am sure she'll be saving it up for a really choice moment. In any case, this appeared to put her in a good mood.

Since things were going well, I decided not to try to bug Rosalind about her grades. I remain very concerned about this, but I do feel like she is making progress in other life areas, and I don't want to mess it up by getting on her back.

I also want to try to have some sort of relationship with Dad, and I have agreed in principle to put my anger about the past aside, but as I sit here tonight, I wonder if I can do it. I guess we will find out.

Any word from Kimberley? (You knew I was going to ask, so there it is.)

—Sean

> > >

Dear Fluffy:

I am back. Niall is hilarious. We spent a long time walking around the neighborhood with Sean being all like "this is where my mom did this, and this is where my mom did that," and he was bumming me out because of course as long as we are on the subject of dead moms, I have two, and I have been doing better and didn't want to get sad right then and even Sean was kind of getting that misty look like he gets watching sappy commercials or whatever. (This was after we walked all over Penn and Sean was all like, look how good college is, of course you need good grades to get in here, blah blah blah like he is being slick or like I'm going to start doing math homework because I saw where dumb kids in sweatshirts eat bad food.)

So I was getting bummed out about even just being there, it started to feel totally unreal, like who the hell am I and why am I walking around Philadelphia with this guy I didn't even know on my last birthday getting this family history lesson about some family I don't even feel like a part of. I started getting all sad and quiet, all just get me home to my room so I can forget about why I'm here, and then Niall starts in with all these stories about here's where this girl lived who tried to cut my dick off when she found me with her sister, here's where I sold weed to the guy who's now the junior senator from a certain state, and stuff like this.

Anyway, it made me forget for a while and actually was pretty entertaining. So then we drove home and Sean and me were talking and I totally thought we were going to hear now don't end up like him, blah blah blah, but it was just much more normal and he was like telling me about how he was still mad which was kind of weird I guess but it wasn't like he wanted me to pat him on the back, it was like he just wanted me to listen which was kind of weird but at the same time it was nice to hear something from him besides you need to shape up blah blah or when my mom died blah blah, and then we just talked about normal stuff and so that was okay.

> > >

IM from Rosalind90

Rosalind90: K8! R U THERE?
Redchordfan03: K8 IS IN THE HOUSE. WHERE R U?
Rosalind90: ALSO IN THE HOUSE. BACK FROM PHILLY. MET DONORBOY'S DAD, MY GRAMPS I GUESS
Redchordfan03: EVIL STONER?
Rosalind90: I LIKED HIM. WAY LESS UPTITE THAN DONORBOY. REALLY FUNNY & HAS LOTS OF FUNNY STORIES ABOUT DEALING WEED TO STUDENTS WHO LATER BECAME SENATORS AND STUFF.

Redchordfan03: COOL. I CALLED JEN.

Rosalind90: AND?

Redchordfan03: SHE IS FINE. I TOLD HER CARSTEN IS A CREEP, SHE WAS ALL HE CARES ABOUT ME, U DON'T, HANG OUT W/YR GOODY GOODY FRIEND THEN, ETC.

Rosalind90: WHAT A BITCH! WEIRD SHE WAS SO NICE TO ME B4.

Redchordfan03: YEAH SHE WAS NICE 2 ME 4 LIKE 9 YRS.

Rosalind90: SORRY.

Redchordfan03: MAKES ME SAD ☹

Rosalind90: ME2.

Redchordfan03: HEY GOOD NEWS THO

Rosalind90: ?

Redchordfan03: DON'T B MAD BUT I GAVE YR POEM 2 MY CUZ & HE LOVES IT & WANTS 2 MAKE A CSRA SONG FROM IT. HOPE ITS OK.

Rosalind90: YEAH! HOPE ITS BETTER THAN THAT SATANS PLAYPEN SONG. ☺

Redchordfan03: BETTER LYRICS ANYWAY ☺

Rosalind90: WANNA GET COFFEE 2MORROW?

Redchordfan03: OK BUT NO DINER.

Rosalind90: COOL. CU 2MORROW.

Redchordfan03: OK BYE.

> > >

Dear Fluffy:

Back from school. Kate told me Jen actually called me a "goody goody *dyke* bitch," and I can't believe that because I thought she was cool, or maybe I can't believe I thought she was cool, I don't know, but I didn't know what to say because I don't know if it's a lie, I mean I might or might not be both of those things so I was like that's so mean just because of my moms and Kate was like yeah and that was like it.

So, Fluffy, believe it or not I have actually been think-ing about my bliss since talking to Niall and I don't know what it is, except I am pretty sure it's not math homework. I like to cook but I don't know if that's my bliss or not. Ap-parently I am a metal songwriter now, which I actually went and told Sean because I was excited because it's my stuff but also because the cute guy will know my name. I left that part out when I talked to Sean, but he was like all enthusiastic, that's great, you could be the metal Robert Hunter and I was like who the hell is that and he said there was some famous hippie stoner band where this guy who wasn't in the band wrote songs. I think the Grateful Dead would be a way better metal name but Sean says they play like stoner country blues or something.

So maybe mistress of metal is my bliss. Maybe being a goody goody bitch is my bliss, but then that would mean math homework, so maybe not. BTW I also gave "Girl in a Cage" to Westerberg for like extra credit or whatever but also because I guess I want somebody grown up to like it and he said he would read it tonight and let me know.

I don't know, Fluffy, I don't know exactly what to do or anything, but I did actually do my history homework tonight because it is not my bliss but sucks less than math and I guess if stupid Jen is going to call me a goody goody bitch I should try to live up to it.

I know she called me a dyke too and I don't know if I should try to live up to that or not. I am bored of thinking

about it, bored of worrying about it but for some reason
being bored of it doesn't actually make it stop. Oh well.

Christmas is coming up, like every store me and Kate
went to today was totally Christmas with the songs playing and the dancing santas and the little bendy santas
which Kate stole two and gave me one so I guess I am an
accessory to a crime, ha ha. I used to love it so much and
now I don't even want it to be Christmas because I am
trying not to think about it but it will be a lot of time
around the house with nothing to think about but being
sad and stupid it's a wonderful life, Zuzu, kids, and
George Bailey the richest man in town which Mom always watched and cried and I don't want to have a stupid
holiday and be sad or worse yet go there there for Karen
even though if she asks me I don't know how I'm going
to say no way.

Maybe I should take like a voke cooking class or something instead of math. I wonder if they let you do that. I
don't know what my bliss is but sleep is looking good right
now.

> > >

Dear Sean and Rosalind,

*I really enjoyed seeing you. I said I would write, so I am
writing. I am not sure what I should say, though, except
that really was the best weekend I have had in a long time.*

*Sean—I meant what I said about you being an old soul
and me being a young one. But I think I probably should*

*have done more to make you want to hang around with me.
You did well without my help, but, for what it's worth, I am
sorry I didn't do more.*

*Rosalind—I could tell from Sean's getting that disap-
proving look every time you laughed at one of my stories
that he was afraid you would follow me into the erstwhile
family business so that you too could have humorous adventures. I think you've got more sense than me (or probably
Sean either)—you seem like a very old soul to me—but I
guess I should balance out what I said with the fact that one
of the reasons I got out of it was that it got too dangerous. I
can laugh about getting shot at now, but at the time I soiled
myself, which was a detail I omitted from the funny version.*

*The novel is almost finished. Some kid who used to come
in the bar every night when he was at Penn is some kind of
literary agent now, so I'm going to send it off to him and see
what happens.*

*I will see you in a couple weeks. Until then, take it easy
on each other.*

—Niall Cassidy, Famous Stoner Grandfather

> > >

Dear Niall,

*Sorry about the free restaurant postcard. I will write a real
letter soon. I just wanted to tell you that the soiling yourself
part actually makes the story funnier. Especially since you
say, "soiled myself" instead of, like, "shit my pants" or*

something. Just for future reference. Also, I have no desire to deal weed.

—Rosalind

> > >

To: Rosalind90@aol.com
From: Sean_Cassidy@publaw.org
Subject: odds and ends

Hey there. So I have several things to say, and I figured that some of them might make you roll your eyes or generally tune out because of excessive corniness, so I thought I would write you instead.

I'll start with the corniest part, but stick with me, because it does get less corny. First of all, I had a very nice time this weekend, and I enjoyed our ride home. I think you are probably correct about Niall and his trying to do his best. It's helpful to me to get the perspective of someone outside the situation.

Also, and prepare to roll your eyes, I am still very happy that you got out of that situation that you probably wisely still refuse to tell me about. My friend Dave is always telling me about how teenagers are supposed to make mistakes and use bad judgment, but this is an instance where you used better judgment than many adults probably would have.

I will add that I know your mothers would have been very proud of you too. Now, before you throw something at the screen (people speaking for the dead has always been one of my pet peeves, especially when people who had no business doing it tried to say something about what my mother would have thought about me), I do have some information to back this up.

Well, I imagine Sandy, from what I knew of her, would have been having some sort of nervous fit such as you have seen me have a few times recently. Eva, though—well, I don't know if this is something I should tell you or not, but it feels like the right thing to do, so here goes. I sanitized somewhat my story of what Eva told me about her years on *Single Dads Club*. Something else she told me was that she left acting and Los Angeles and went to dental school because she was terrified of making bad decisions. She did not get too specific, but she said she was "young and stupid and rich," and that she was "afraid my life was going in a very bad direction."

So when I say that she would be proud of you, it's because she also took steps to get herself out of a bad situation, but when she was a full nine years older than you are now. I am admittedly very new to this parenting thing, but I do believe that one thing all parents want is for their children to make better decisions than they did.

All right. On to a totally different subject. We tossed around the idea of your taking that voke cooking class that meets at the same time as your math class. I am not trying to impose this particular brand of bliss on you, but I did decide to explore this possibility. I exchanged e-mails with your math teacher, who appears to be an incredible pain in the ass. In any case, she informed me in the same e-mail that it is "nearly mathematically impossible" for you to pass for the year and that she was "categorically opposed" to your taking another class. Apparently she believes you need to suffer for six more months for your unpardonable sin of not being enthralled by quadratic equations. She assured me that she would "fight such a move every step of the way."

Call me a lawyer, but this does sound like a challenge to me. I'll be happy to take it on, but, again, I don't want to squash this woman just for my own ego gratification. No, that's a lie. I couldn't stand her tone and would derive great ego gratification from getting this to happen, but I do recognize that this is ultimately about you and not me. So let me know if this is something you want, and I will make sure you get it. (And should we meet with Dr. Vanian, you could create a bingo card for me with the words "hostile environment" in every square and probably win in about thirty seconds.)

Finally, and I suppose this is another eye-roller, I think you should consider re-joining that peer counseling group. You've been through a great deal and appear to be putting it back together, and your pugilistic adventures would surely give you credibility with even the most hardened students. Just a thought.

See you at dinner.

—Sean

>>>

To: Sean_Cassidy@publaw.org
From: Rosalind90@aol.com
Subject: Re: odds and ends

Sean—I don't know if I wanted to know that about Mom but it does kind of explain why she never really talked about being on TV and didn't have any tapes of the show or anything. Anyway, thanks, I guess. I mean, I don't know. I need to think about it, but I guess you're right that it's something that's good for me to know. Maybe. I swear I can't picture Mom as some kind of hard partyer who needs to leave town. I am actually not sure I want to. But whatever, I guess she would have told me eventually.

I don't know if cooking is my bliss either (Niall is such a corndog with that phrase. I guess the apple doesn't fall far from the tree, ha-ha) but math class is not. I actually think Ms. Weymouth is okay, but if I can't possibly pass I guess I'd rather do just about anything else and then do math in summer school. I guess I'd rather cook than cut class and smoke in the bathroom. (That is a joke. Kind of.)

By the way I think I will not be home for dinner if it's okay. I mean, um, can I go out? Kate is going to see Child Soldiers Run Amok practice in her cousin Jamie's basement and I guess they are going to do my song, or whatever the song they made from my poem. Like I told you the band is straight edge so caffeine will be the strongest thing there. And it's at 85 Boylston Street right here in Charlesborough, and Jamie's mom's phone number is 617-555-1824 if you really want to call and embarrass me, but just please don't talk about Metallica with anybody. Kate says they will get pizza or something so I will get fed and I will be home by 8.

—Rosalind

> > >

New text message!
From: Sean
3:43 pm
U R THE HI PRIESTESS OF METAL. GO & HAVE FUN. I DID CALL BUT SAID
ZIP ABOUT METALLICA.

> > >

To: Rosalind90@aol.com
From: Karenzallrite@msn.com
Subject: Hello?

Rosalind—Since you have not been answering my phone calls or
returning my voice mails, I thought I should try e-mail. I hope that
you are just busy and happy doing teenager things, but I am concerned about you and would appreciate it if you would check in. I
know that Thanksgiving was tough, and that holidays in general are
going to be tough for a while. I understand if talking to me pulls
you back into that mindset, but I would really appreciate an e-mail
telling me that you are all right. Or, if you are not all right, an e-
mail telling me that Lisa is helping you and that you are not making bad choices.

 I feel an obligation to your moms to keep up with you, but,
more than that, you are important to me. I was thinking maybe
we could go out to dinner sometime this week—I will spring for
something fancy, and I will promise not to cry. What do you say?

—Karen

   > > >

To: Sean_Cassidy@publaw.org
From: davidsanders@Newcastle.k12.mass.edu
Subject: Re: My big weekend

Hey. I don't have anything to tell you about your old man. As you
know, my relationship with my own is not in the greatest shape,
so I will just say I feel your pain on this issue and leave it at that.

But you don't really give a shit what I say about that, because you gave the game away with your little "offhand" question about Kimberley. I swear to God, I've known you for fifteen years and you think you can fool me with something that lame?

Okay, so Allie told me that Kimberley called her and said that you "give good e-mail," which somehow feels more disgusting than it actually is. And Allie says she thinks Kimberley has a crush on you. There. Happy? "Gives good e-mail." Jesus. If I get out of this without puking, it will be some kind of miracle.

By the way, Kimberley arrives in thirty-two days, if you want to start making little x's on your little calendar.

—Dave

> > >

Dear Fluffy,

I have actually been too busy to write, which I guess is good. I went with Kate to Child Soldiers Run Amok practice, and it was kind of embarrassing because they were all telling me how much they like my lyrics or whatever, and the cute lead singer was like, oh, you are so talented, how long have you been writing, blah blah, and I had to make something up because I didn't want to be like I used to write a lot of poems in middle school but I haven't written anything in six months but I still pulled out something better than Satan's Playpen.

So then Kate and I sat there like these total groupies which I guess we are except for without the having sex with the band part and they played a bunch of songs in-

cluding "Satan's Playpen" and "Girl in a Cage" which totally rocks if I do say so myself. Not that I had anything to
do with the rocking part, but I felt really proud and excited and kind of happy even though Ash the lead singer
was paying way more attention to Kate than me which
okay she is two years older and way better looking and
actually has boobs but is not the high priestess of metal
which is what Sean called me.

But anyway, it was fun. I talked to Lisa the next day
and she was like this is so good for you, and I was kind of
like did you hear the part about how I was all jealous of
my best friend, but she was like, well, you have something
else that you can call your own besides your grief.

I don't know. It's one poem that some guys who write
bad lyrics for themselves decided to use for a song. It's kind
of like Sean getting all into the cooking—everybody
wants me to find my Bliss but I am just trying stuff. Well,
whatever. It's way better than everybody being freaked out
about how I am wrecking my life.

And speaking of which I am out of math class which
I guess means no early decision to Harvard, ha ha, even
though Sean when I said that said no you just write some
essay about how much you learned from your grief and
blah blah and they will ignore this year. Which would be
okay if I wanted to go to Harvard but I totally don't.

Went out to dinner with Karen which means I guess
Sean ate frozen burritos again. I was pretty afraid that she
was going to be all weepy or whatever, but we just talked
about stuff and she did give me the vagina power speech
but it was way less painful than I thought it might be. It

was actually kind of nice, I mean, whatever, it's not like
I'm going to talk to Sean about this (anyway, what does he
know, he just beat off into a cup, which is actually just as
gross or maybe grosser even than thinking about moms
having sex), so it was nice to feel like I could maybe talk to
Karen or ask her something and she wouldn't freak out on
me. But I did want to make her a bingo card that said "sex
positive feminism" on it because I guess that is the official
name for vagina power.

So I am having a good week Fluffy which is I guess
an occasion but of course I am still worried because both
Karen and Sean are starting to make noises about Christmas, which I totally don't want them to have their stupid
tug of war over me again and also stupid holidays are
going to remind me of everything. I kind of just wish I
could skip it completely, just pretend it's not happening,
but I guess even if I could get Sean and Karen to agree I
am going to see George Bailey every time I turn on the
TV so oh well.

I don't know. I feel like some good stuff is starting
to happen—like no more math homework until summer
school, which I wasn't going to do any anyway, but now I
can stop feeling guilty about it—and I think Christmas is
just going to screw me up again, like I am just going to fall
right back to punching the shit out of hockey players or
something. Maybe I should write a metal song about
punching hockey players.

> > >

To: Karenzallrite@msn.com
From: Sean_Cassidy@publaw.org
Subject: Xmas

Hello! Well, I am writing with my Rosalind update. As you may or
may not know, Rosalind is some kind of heavy metal songwriter
now, as a band known as Child Soldiers Run Amok has put one of
her poems to music. She showed me the poem—it's pretty alarm-
ingly dark, but I am taking the point of view that if she can work
those feelings out in verse, she'll stop punching hockey players.

In any case, I am eagerly awaiting the demo CD with the song
on it.

I spoke to Rosalind's math teacher, who informed me that Rosalind could only pass if she got nothing but 100's for the rest of
the year, which seems incredibly unlikely, so I did some persuading
with the administration to get Rosalind into a cooking class during
that period. She is going to do math in summer school. Apologies
if she's told you all or any of this. What I have noticed in the last
week or so is that Rosalind seems to be doing very well—that is
to say, while she still retreats to her room early and often, she no
longer appears to be moping around constantly. When she learned
that the band was going to use her poem, she came out of her
room smiling and practically jumping around—happy and enthusiastic in a way that I have read about in Eva's letters but never seen
personally before then. It was a really wonderful moment.

I'd love to hear what you've noticed recently, or if you got any
pertinent information at dinner the other night. I'd also like to
know what kind of plans you are making for Christmas. My father is
coming to town, and I am in the process of trying to set things up,
and I thought you and I should touch base around this issue so

that we don't end up with overlapping and competing plans.
Thanks, and I will talk to you soon.

—Sean

> > >

To: Sean_Cassidy@publaw.org
From: Karenzallrite@msn.com
Subject: Re: Xmas

Sean,
Thank you for the update. I would say that Rosalind seemed upbeat
and chatty at dinner the other night in a way that reminded me of
her old self. I am optimistic. I have mixed feelings about the whole
poetry/metal thing. You know how I feel about the negativity in
that music, but I am glad that something made Rosalind happy. I
hope it's a phase and there are no skull tattoos on the horizon.

Thanks for asking about Christmas. I have once again ducked out
of the family gathering in Cincinnati, so obviously want to see Rosalind during this time. As you might know, Sandy and Eva always
threw a well-attended Christmas dinner, and I do think it would be
good for Rosalind and, yes, me too, for her to have access to that
tradition.

I have, in the past, taken one for the team in the name of main-
taining this tradition: Once I sat next to this guy Raoul who—well,
had we not been at Christmas dinner, I think I would have forsaken
my nonviolent convictions and strangled him. Indeed, though you
and I have had our moments, I would rather share a desert island
with you than another meal with him.

The spirit of the meal, though of course it was not explicitly Christian, was always one of goodwill and forgiveness, and so if you'd like for the three, or, I suppose, four of us to do Christmas together, I think that would be a good addition to the tradition.

Jesus, that's a really backhanded invitation. I mean it as an olive branch, but I'm not very good at this stuff. So let's all do Christmas together, assuming you want to.

—Karen

> > >

Dear Dad,

Thanks for your letter, and I am sorry it has taken me so long to respond. I hope you are still planning to come up for Christmas. You made quite an impression on Rosalind. She has been talking a great deal about "following her bliss." She always says it sarcastically, but she says it so often that I believe she is really pondering it. I will say, also, that I enjoyed seeing you and having a real conversation and perhaps beginning to build a relationship as adults. I appreciate the apology, and I promise not to batter you with my old resentments as long as you live up to your end of the Tarkus bargain.

Speaking of music, Rosalind's bliss apparently includes being a songwriter, as some metal band that her friend's cousin is in put one of her poems to music. The words are alarming, and the music is something I might have enjoyed when I was sixteen that just made me grind my teeth. I sup-

pose that is the point. The poem is depressing and seems to me a pretty transparent metaphor for the author. (It's called "Girl in a Cage." I am reminded about how John Lennon said he eventually figured out that he'd written "Crippled Inside" about himself. Well, perhaps comparing Rosalind to John Lennon indicates wishful thinking about her musical prospects, but I think the song is more about her than she realizes.) I am not concerned about the depressing lyrical content, though—in some strange way, it seems healthy to me. Healthier, anyway, than breaking the noses of hockey players. (Did I tell you about that? Did she? Quite a story.)

I bullied the school and got her taken out of math class and put into cooking class. She will not tell me anything about cooking class. I have no idea what to make of this information, but I am assuming she would tell me if she hated it.

Well, it is late at night and I suppose I should go to bed so that I can properly bully school systems in the morning. I have made plans for us to have Christmas dinner with Karen, who is Rosalind's "aunt" I told you about. She drives me nuts, but I am going to suck it back for Ros's sake. Perhaps that is the mark of a real family. In any case, I am glad you are coming for a number of reasons, but not the least of which is that I will just feel more comfortable at Karen's house if I feel like I have an ally, which I hope is what you are. In any case, I will see you next week. Maybe you can bring the novel. I'd love to see it, if you're willing to show it.

Love,
Sean

> > >

Dear Fluffy,

Okay, well, school has been out for 2 days and I am losing my fucking mind here, it's like I can't stay in this house but I can't go anywhere, I hate Christmas so much I want to scream. Apparently we are all going to have Christmas dinner at Karen's house, which is just, I am afraid she's gonna cry again, I am going to be jealous that Sean was able to get one parent back anyway, I am going to scream.

No, it will be fine.

No, it won't. I feel twitchy, like I am going to jump out of my skin or something. Which I guess is kind of nicer than feeling flat, or different anyway, but I am afraid it's coming back, like I am just holding it back and the dam is going to break and I am going to be the one crying before Karen can even start, like where the hell are my mommies if this is Christmas, why the hell can they even have it, they should just cancel it or get some green guy to steal it or something.

I watched that on TV last night and had to go to my room and cry because I don't even know why because I want to kick Cindy Lou Who's ass, I want to get out of my skin and go live in somebody else's, somebody normal, somebody who can just be happy on a happy day instead of losing their mind, or anyway just getting jittery and sad and fuck this.

The thing is nobody asked me shit about Christmas. Sean and Karen all worked this thing out, we're gonna pretend we don't hate each other for one day, so we can be like a family or whatever, but nobody asked me and I don't want to have Christmas because my fucking family is dead! I don't want any of it!

Shit. Fluffy you are not helping me tonight, I am just getting worse, because before I was jittery and now I am jittery but I have these tears rolling down my face and I can't do it Fluffy, I can't have stupid Christmas without my moms, I can't do it, I won't do it. Good night.

> > >

IM from Rosalind90

Rosalind90: K8?

Redchordfan03: IN THE HIZZOUSE

Rosalind90: CANT SLEEP. Y R U AWAKE?

Redchordfan03: I NEVER SLEEP. SLEEP IS 4 THE WEAK!

Rosalind90: IM GLAD U R UP. I M SAD, FREAKING OUT, CRYING, BASICALLY A MESS.

Redchordfan03: Y?

Rosalind90: XMAS, DEAD MOMS, SAME OLD SAME OLD. I MISS THEM REALLY BAD AND EVERYTHING XMAS REMINDS ME, CANT STAND IT. XMAS SEEMS WRONG WITHOUT THEM.

Redchordfan03: SORRY. XMAS SUCKS HERE TOO. TOYS 4 TWINS, LUMP O COAL 4 ME IF I GET ANYTHING, EVERYBODY LOOKS AT ME LIKE THEY WANT ME 2 LEAVE.

Rosalind90: HATE IT CANT STAND BEING ME I JUST WISH I COULD RUN AWAY NOT DO XMAS. I WAS OK FOR LIKE 2 DAYS, NOW IM AFRAID IM GONNA GET SAD AGAIN 4EVER.

Redchordfan03: ☹

Rosalind90: FREAKING OUT, CAN'T DEAL. REGULAR DAYS R OK, BUT XMAS IS NOT OK AT ALL.

Redchordfan03: WANNA LEAVE, GO C UR MOM ON TV?

Rosalind90: ?

Redchordfan03: GOOGLED HER SHOW, THEY HAVE 4 EPISODES AT SOME TV MUSEUM IN NYC.

Rosalind90: IVE NEVER SEEN IT. IT MIGHT MAKE ME SAD. BUT THEN I AM SAD ALREADY.

Redchordfan03: ILL BOOST MOMS CREDIT CARD, BRING MY ID SO WE CAN STAY IN A HOTEL.

Rosalind90: IT SOUNDS COMPLETELY INSANE BUT I DAMN SURE CANT STAY HERE.

Redchordfan03: THERES A BUS FROM CHINATOWN AT 6 A.M. IT COSTS 15 BUCKS. MEET ME THERE.

Rosalind90: UM . . .

Rosalind90: OK. MEET U AT THE CHINATOWN T STOP AT 5:45.

Redchordfan03: THIS WILL ROCK! BEST XMAS EVER!

Rosalind90: YEAH. C U IN 4 HOURS!

> > >

Dear Sean,

Good morning. I am sorry, I mean I actually am sorry because I know that I am going to tell you not to worry and you are going to worry anyway, but really you shouldn't.

Basically I can't deal with Christmas, so I am running away. From Christmas. Not from you. I appreciate everything you have done with school and the food and with everything, I mean, you are doing a good job really, it's just

that you are not my moms, and Christmas without them feels
wrong, and I don't want to talk about it, I don't want to sit in
my room and cry, I don't want to sit there eating Tofurky
and pretending that I am happy because I am really sad.

This kind of freaks me out because I thought I was done
being sad, but whatever. So, anyway, I am leaving town for
two days. I do not have suicidal ideation and I am not going
to hurt myself or any hockey players. That is a "Rosalind
almost got expelled" joke. I just can't be here, I just can't do
Christmas.

I will be back, and probably you will be mad and
ground me, and Karen will yell at me and cry about how
could I do this to her, but I'm really not doing this to any-
body. I just have to do it for myself. I am with Kate and we
have money and a place to stay and I will not end up like
some girl in a Lifetime movie or something. I'm just kind of
taking an unexpected vacation.

Like I said, I am sorry, but I guess not sorry enough not
to do it, but anyway, please don't worry because I am fine.
Say hi to Niall for me and tell him I am sorry I missed him.

Hee Haw and Merry Christmas,
Rosalind

> > >

Dear Fluffy,
I am on the Lucky Wah bus and we are somewhere in
Connecticut. Kate is asleep which I can't believe because
she had that gigantic coffee from Dunkin Donuts, and also

I am here clackity clack clacking on the keyboard because I brought you along Fluffy so that Sean would not read you and try to figure out where I am which you know he would do.

I am wicked smart except that I did actually forget to turn my phone off, so I had to just not answer when he called because I am afraid I'd feel guilty and go back or tell him where I am or something, so I turned it off and put it in my bag. So apparently we are going to New York to watch *Single Dads Club,* which is completely stupid but what the hell. Kate said she is sure that the museum is open on December 24th, which if it isn't I am going to beat her like a hockey player, no I will just maybe order room service or something. I don't know, Fluffy, this is a crazy thing to do, like a totally crazy thing, but whatever, maybe I am totally crazy. Anyway I felt totally crazy at two in the morning, and now I just feel kind of crazy and I want to just have fun and not worry about who is worrying, but I am finding that hard while Kate snoozes and everybody else talks in Chinese and occasionally looks over here like they have never seen a girl with red hair before which maybe they haven't.

Anyway I am tired too because I totally didn't sleep last night and so maybe I will try to nap before we get to NYC because what the hell else can I do.

> > >

To: Rosalind90@aol.com
From: Sean_Cassidy68@yahoo.com
Subject: Hee Haw and Merry Christmas

Ros,

Are you checking e-mail? Will you check my text messages? My voice mails? Will my wireless modem card work so I can send this? I am plagued with questions.

First and foremost, of course, is this: Where are you?

That is to say, I have deduced that you are in New York City, which, as near as I can determine, narrows my search area down to a few square miles and a few million people.

You didn't really think I was going to sit home and have Christmas with Dad and not worry about you, did you? Do you understand that this is just not how families operate?

Actually, I shouldn't say that, because this does appear to be how Kate's family operates, to some degree. By now I hope you have discovered that Kate's mom has canceled her credit cards. She definitely appeared to be more concerned with their disappearance than Kate's. We spoke only briefly (I got the number from the metal bassist himself, who said, "Geez, I hope they're okay. That was a dumb thing to do."), but she told me twice of "the light Emma and Madison have brought to our lives," which simultaneously annoyed the hell out of me and explained a great deal about Kate's willingness to bug out for Christmas.

Yours, though, remains a mystery to me. Am I like that in some way? I suppose I must be not giving you something you need. You said in your note that you couldn't do Christmas. Did it occur to you to mention this to me? Do you think I don't understand how hard Christmas is?

I'm sorry—I appear to be berating you. Perhaps I won't send this at all. Well, I suppose there isn't any harm in writing it, since even if I did decide to send it, the likelihood that I could get my phone and modem to work together at the same time is even smaller than the likelihood that you are eagerly checking e-mail wherever you are.

But I don't know what else to do. I miss you, I am worried about you, I am so angry at you I could scream. I suppose ultimately I feel betrayed—that I have tried in every way I know how to show love and care for you, and you just spit in my face with this kind of be-havior.

Well, that is petulant. In that case, I am definitely not sending this. In which case, can I tell you that if anything has happened to you, I am going to throw myself under this train. I suppose this is next to impossible to understand at age fourteen, but I can't imagine that my life would be worth living if you came to harm while you were under my care. Somehow the fact that I have been this worried twice before and everything ended up coming out fine is not consoling me.

Well. Indulging my petulance isn't helping me. Where are you? How on earth can I find you? Dad promised to scour the lowlife hot spots (you've scotched his Christmas plans too, by the way), but even now I believe you have more sense than that. What is in New York that you want to see? Surely if you just wanted to hole up in a Red Roof Inn, you could have done that somewhere that was within reach of the commuter rail, and your Lucky Wah adventure would not have been necessary. (If I may digress, I am very proud of the way we figured that out—got the ATM address where Kate used the purloined card—and yes, I did feel a twinge of affection for your friend because her pain-in-the-ass mother had no idea how

Kate might have gotten the PIN) and, with the help of Karen's incredibly rusty Cantonese from her ESL days in Hong Kong (interesting story, actually—do you know it?), we found that you went
to New York.

I will digress, since you're never going to read this anyway, and
say that a positive side effect of this, assuming we find you alive
and unharmed, is that Karen and I have had some time on the train
to talk, reconcile, whatever. Anyway, I am feeling a great deal less
antagonism toward her than I used to. She is also worried to death
about you, though you probably know that and selfishly choose to
disregard that. Ah, there's my anger peeking through again.

Karen, by the way, postulates that this little adventure may be
some sort of you getting in touch with your sexuality romantic
getaway. Did I do anything to make you believe that it would be
necessary to run away for that?

Well, I suppose that's immaterial, as I don't believe that expla-
nation, because I do actually believe that you told me the truth in
your note. Which I believe because I believe that we have built trust
between us. Which is why I can't understand why you did this.
Well, I appear to be going around in circles. And you are going . . .
where? Forty minutes to Penn Station. Hopefully I'll figure it
out.

Love,
Sean Cassidy

       > > >

To: davidsanders@Newcastle.k12.mass.edu
From: Sean_Cassidy68@yahoo.com
Subject: It's an interesting life

Dave,
Guess where I am?

You, as I write this, are out there having fun in the warm California sun, while I am in New York. Why, you might ask, am I not enjoying, or at least tolerating, the neo-family Christmas I had planned?

Well, this is because Rosalind ran away to New York. I got up on Christmas Eve day and found this note from Rosalind saying that she was safe, she was fine, and I was not to interpret this as a rejection of me, but she was running away from Christmas for a few days. She assured me that she would not end up like a girl "in a Lifetime movie," but naturally that is what I feared.

Some detective work ensued, but, to make a long story short, I found that she and her friend Kate had gone to New York, and so I ended up taking the Acela to New York with Karen and meeting my dad at Penn Station so that the three of us could scour the city.

Dad felt the most comfortable and had the most contacts in the kinds of places where scared runaways end up getting evil pimps to buy them drinks, so he volunteered to scour those sections. I didn't really think he'd have any luck, because I was sure, in spite of the evidence, that Ros had more sense than that.

Karen was convinced that Ros and her friend Kate had run away for some kind of proto-lesbian romantic getaway, so she volunteered for the gay bookstores, bars, etc. I didn't really think that was what was going on either, so that left me to search . . . where?

Unlike Dad and Karen, I had no clues in my own biography as to where they might be. I did know, though, that Kate is an artist, so I decided to hit some museums. I went to the Met, where I paid a fortune, walked around not even noticing the stuff on the wall, had an interesting conversation with the head of security, and did not find them. The place was so huge, though, that I could have missed them.

Back down to MOMA, which also cost a fortune, and which also proved fruitless, though the head of security was very accommodating and allowed me to peer at all the monitors, thus saving me the trouble of tromping around and seeing masterpieces I would be unable to appreciate. I stood there for about twenty minutes, trying to follow the action on a bank of dozens of monitors. My eyes hurt, and I still hadn't found them.

By this point, I was getting discouraged and—well, I will leave it to you to imagine my anxiety level. You have certainly seen me at that level before, but the anxiety spiked with dread is a particularly heinous variation.

I began walking aimlessly around, and I spoke to Sandy and Eva—you know, something along the lines of, "Goddammit, if there is any way for you to do anything here, I really need some fucking help!"

I got nothing in response. But then I turned the corner, and I saw the Museum of Television and Radio, which I had never heard of and knew nothing about. And, now, you will mock me, and you probably should, but I knew immediately that that is where they were. I do not know whether Sandy and Eva's ghosts responded to my profane incantations or whether it was just the fact that I had just tried to contact them . . . well, to backtrack, Rosalind and I had bonded earlier over our inability to feel the presence of dead loved ones at their grave sites, and I thought, if there is any *Single Dads Club* memorabilia or anything in this place, that might be a way to at least get some kind of contact with Eva, if not Sandy, and I suppose one is better than zero.

I went in looking for the exhibit halls, only to find that there aren't any. A frustrating conversation with an intern led to a more productive conversation with the head of security (and may I say God bless these fine men and women who I have perhaps in the past derided as rent-a-cops, as they were uniformly sympathetic, patient, and helpful at all three museums) and a trip to the library, where you can order up old episodes of thousands of shows to watch in a little carrel in a very dim room.

And there, huddled in a carrel, watching *Single Dads Club*, faces lit blue from the TV, were Ros and Kate. Ros was crying, her shoulders heaving up and down, and Kate was rubbing her back. In view of your "birth of Max" sappiness, I will try to restrain what I commit to zeroes and ones here, but all my anger simply evaporated from my body as I saw this poor kid weeping at the sight of this incredibly terrible sitcom.

Of course I started to cry too, from relief, from love, from empathy, whatever. So I approach the sobbing teen with tears running down my own cheek, and I just sat down next to them and asked if I could watch too.

Kate was nice enough to volunteer her headphones, and Ros— I am getting all choked up as I write this, so I will do it quickly— leaned over and said, "I'm sorry Sean, I'm really sorry, I suck, I'm sorry."

"It's okay," I said, and I put my arm around her shoulder, and she did not shrug away, tell me to get the fuck off, or anything.

And we watched the end of the episode. Which, as luck would

have it, was the final episode, the one I had never seen, where Tracey decides to go to college instead of going off to Europe with her shady boyfriend.

It made me so sad to see Eva there, twenty-two or whatever she was, and everything just overwhelmed me: sadness for Eva and for Sandy, sadness for Ros, sadness for little me watching that show in the dark and missing my mom. I guess we made quite a picture there, both of our shoulders bobbing up and down as tears ran down our cheeks, which I suppose is especially ironic given that this was one of those "very special episodes" that I assume the writers hope will inspire that kind of emotion but that always end up just being stupid.

Well, there we are. All five of us are in a hotel here somewhere in Midtown, and it is Christmas Day, and as strange as it sounds, because I'm crying again as I write this, I am as happy as I have ever been.

—Sean

> > >

Single Dads Club
Episode 2-22
"Tracey's Decision, Part 2"

Act Three

Establishing shot: CINCINNATI SKYLINE at dusk
EXT-JIM and GARY'S HOUSE at dusk
Cut to INT-LIVING ROOM

(*GARY* sits alone on the couch, staring at the phone. Enter
CHIP, in Cincinnati Reds cap, and *JIM*, in worn "Cincinnati
Reds, 1976 World Champions" T-shirt.)

CHIP

Hey there, Uncle Gary. Hear anything from Miss
European Traveler yet?

GARY

Do I look like I've heard anything?

CHIP

No, you look more like you can't believe you ate
the whole thing.
(*JIM* swats *CHIP* on the back of the head, knocking off his
baseball cap.)

CHIP

Ow! Child abuse!

JIM

No, making you watch the Reds' bullpen was
child abuse. That was just good old parental
discipline. Go up to your room for a minute. I
wanna talk to Uncle Gary.

CHIP

(*exiting, rubbing the back of his head*)
I've said it before, and I'll say it again—you guys are
over your heads. This place needs a woman's touch.

JIM

With a mouth like that, that kid'll be lucky to get
a woman's touch by the time he's thirty.

(*JIM* sits on the couch next to *GARY*.)

JIM

She'll do the right thing, Gare. She's a good kid.

GARY

Well, she always has been. But that was before she
met this hippie beatnik kid. He keeps telling her to
follow her bliss, but I've got a good idea he wants
her to follow his bliss right into the back of his
van. Times like this I miss Carol like crazy. I can't
help feeling like if she were alive, she'd know
what to do, she'd know what to say, she'd help me.

JIM

Yeah. Whereas times like this I couldn't be
happier that Cass walked out on me. Oh, wait,
that's every waking minute of every day, and some
when I'm asleep, too.

(Beat. *GARY* doesn't smile.)

JIM

Sorry, Gare. Just trying to make you laugh.

GARY

Keep trying. Maybe you could abuse Chip some
more.

JIM

That would be a giggle, but that kid's such a
jailhouse lawyer, he'll have Child Protective
Services in here if I so much as send him to bed
without dinner. Stubborn kid.

(Enter *TRACEY*.)

GARY

And speaking of which . . .

JIM

(*in exaggerated loud voice*)

Well, yeah, so that Reds bullpen is a real drag!
Hard to believe the Big Red Machine has come to
this! Those guys couldn't find the strike zone with
a map! Well, I'm going to go commiserate with
poor Chip—you know how heartbroken he gets
after a Reds loss. He'll probably be up there for
hours. Or (*looks at* TRACEY) as long as it, um,
takes. Okay! Bullpen troubles.

(*JIM* gets up from the couch.)

JIM

Oh, Tracey, I didn't see you there! I'm off to
console Chip.

(*He exits.*)

(*TRACEY* sits on the couch next to *GARY*.)

TRACEY

Uncle Jim is a really terrible liar.

GARY

Well, maybe you could give him some lessons.

TRACEY

I guess I deserve that.

GARY

You're breaking my heart here, Trace. You know?
Sneaking out, then telling me you're not going to
college? I mean, since Mom died, I've really been
trying, you know? I mean, I've done the best I
could, and I know I wasn't around much before,
but I have been trying to do what I thought Mom
would have done, and I just feel like I've let her
down. Like if she was here this wouldn't be
happening.

(Cut to CHIP, at the top of the steps, peering through the
banister. Cut back to GARY and TRACEY on the couch.)

TRACEY

Well, I guess that's true, Dad. I mean, if Mom was
alive, I probably wouldn't think that I should live
it up while I can, I probably wouldn't think that it
could all end any minute, that I should stay out of
the rat race and do what I want. I probably would
have just gone to college without ever thinking
about it.

(Cut to steps. JIM's face appears next to CHIP's. JIM begins
to pull CHIP by the ear. Cut back to GARY and TRACEY.)

GARY

But, Trace, you know she would have wanted you
to go to college.

(Cut to steps. *JIM* and *CHIP* now both peer through the
banister, obviously not moving until this is over. Cut back to
GARY and *TRACEY.*)

TRACEY

No, Dad, that's what *you* want. You don't know
what Mom would want, and neither do I, because
she's gone.

GARY

Okay, it's what I want. I guess I hoped that would
be enough.

TRACEY
(*eyes filling up*)

It is.

GARY

You mean?

TRACEY

I mean (*pausing to wipe her tears with a tissue she's
gotten from her purse*), I did some thinking about
it. About what I really want for my life, about
whether I really want to go to college, or whether
I'm just going along with the rat race.

(Cut to steps. *CHIP* rolls his eyes, holds his hand in the air, making the "blah blah blah" gesture. *JIM* wears a sad smile as tears run down his cheeks.)

> TRACEY
>
> And what I decided was that because I want to live my life to the fullest, because I want to do what's best with my life, and because I would have wanted Mom to be proud of me, but more than that, because I want *you* to be proud of me, I'm going to college.

> GARY
> (*crying and hugging* TRACEY)
> Oh, honey, that's . . . that's . . .

(Cut to steps.)

> JIM
>
> That's five bucks, Chip-O. I told you she'd make the right decision.

> CHIP
> (*handing over the five bucks*)
> Aw, man! (*Yelling down to* TRACEY) Thanks a lot! He gave me three-to-one odds!

(Pull back to reveal *JIM* and *CHIP* sheepishly coming down the steps.)

> GARY
>
> Hey, thanks a lot for the privacy, guys.

CHIP

I'm sorry, Uncle Gare, but there was money at
stake! Dad gave me three-to-one that she'd go to
college! I could have bought a lot of *Star Wars*
cards with that much cash! You know how it is
when the stakes are high!

GARY

I sure do, Chip. (*Beat. Looks at* TRACEY.) I sure do.

(CUE END THEME.)

Everybody needs somebody
I guess what they say is true
I never thought it would come to this but
I need you

> > >

Dear Fluffy:
Zuzu! Kids! I'm back in Boston!

I am in deep shit of course but that was predictable
so where should I start, I don't know, I guess I finally saw
Single Dads Club, and it made me wicked sad, just incredibly sad, it was so unfair that she was there alive, walking
and talking and not alive like I ever knew her, but alive
anyway, and she's just saying the stupid shit they wrote for
her, not going like, "I love you Ros, you're gonna be OK" or
anything, which I know I didn't expect, not really, I don't
know what the hell I expected. I just wanted to see her.

And there she was, alive on tv but dead really and

never coming back to me and it's one thing to remember
her but to see her face and hear her voice talking was too
much, way worse even than reading her words in the
black album, and I just sat there and cried through three
episodes, and I don't even really know if they were good
or crappy or what the stories were.

But the best part was that Kate just sat there with me
and didn't try to get me to stop crying and didn't tell me it
was okay or she was sorry or anything, she was just there,
and that was the right thing to do.

And then all of a sudden Sean was there too, and he
was all crying, which made me feel a lot worse than if he
had been yelling at me, and so I was like I'm sorry and he
was like, it's okay, and we watched the end of the show
which of course was some sappy thing with Tracey and her
dad and that made me even sadder, like, I don't know, was
that Mom telling me that I do have a dad or something, or
should you get your life lessons from TV or is that something stupid people do? I don't know but Sean suddenly
being there in the dark kind of made the whole thing sadder but also okay and he didn't tell me it was okay either,
because it's not fucking okay, it's never going to be okay,
but he just kind of gave me this half hug and that was
okay and I didn't tell him to get off because it was nice.

After our four episodes of *Single Dads Club* were over,
we had to give up our space at the tv, and we all went back
to the hotel, and Karen met us there and so did Niall and I
felt really bad again for fucking up everybody's Christmas,
and it was worse because even Karen didn't yell at me
about how could I do this to her, so I felt like a toad.

But whatever, I was like I guess we should go get on the Lucky Wah or whatever, and Niall was like well, it's late and we already paid for the rooms, so let's just stay. He said he used to sell weed to some kid who inherited his family's Chinese restaurant or something, and he'd get them to make us a vegetarian feast off the menu, so we did, all five of us with the spinning thing in the middle of the table, and it was cool. Of course Niall joined the Kate fan club but guys of any age seem to love her, but even Karen was kind of smiling and got into this long thing about negativity and catharsis in art and Kate was right there and I didn't understand much of it and just ate my dumplings.

Christmas we just walked around and looked at lights and whatever, and Sean was like I got you all this All-Clad cookware but it's at home, and I was like thanks, not knowing what that meant but Karen told me it was "seriously high-end cookware." Anyway, whatever, it was a nice Christmas, I mean, I did feel kind of better after doing all that crying, and I was laughing a lot with Niall and Kate and Karen and even Sean who is pretty funny when he is not being uptight. Now we are back, and school starts in a week, and Kate is grounded until she dies and so am I, but Sean was like you can still call her and IM her and whatever because of course he loves her but I don't know I guess he loves me too.

We are looking at a new year, and I don't know, it sounds dumb because it's just another day, but I feel like maybe I could have some kind of life that is new and fucked up compared to the old one but not so horrible. I mean I really did feel kinda like I had a family there for a few days, which between Sean and Karen and Niall and Kate is a collection of pretty interesting and screwed up people, and I guess add me on the screwed up part, and maybe even the interesting part too since I am the Mistress of Metal and Queen of the All-Clad.

I don't know, Fluffy. I still hate what happened, and it's not like I wouldn't trade this life for my old one in a second. It is never going to be okay that they died, because it was stupid and wrong and unfair and it hurts, and that's never ever going to be okay. But maybe I will be.

ABOUT THE AUTHOR

BRENDAN HALPIN is the author of the acclaimed memoirs *It Takes a Worried Man* and *Losing My Faculties*. He lives in Boston with his daughter, Rowen.